Written by Shira Amour
Illustrated by Marcus Jeffery

Copyright© 2023

Author	Shira Amour
Publisher	Little Virtuosities, LLC
ISBN	9780578376493
Cover Art / illustrations:	2023© Marcus Jeffery
Author's Photo	2022© Kristina Martin Photography

Dedication

I dedicate this book to my children who I love tremendously and are my everyday inspiration. I pray that you all thrive and live a life full of joy, peace and purpose. To my loving husband who selflessly gave me the support required to follow my passion to write - all while in the midst of us raising a young and very active family together. To my village of support – I cannot express how much I appreciate your acts of kindness. Thank you for every time you chose to be there.

CHARITY

"Hey! Stop right there!" The security guard yelled as he ran out of the trendy women's clothing store. "Stop them! Thieves! Stop right now!"

The two girls squealed, clenched their overstuffed purses, and ran full speed towards the mall entrance. It was a busy Saturday, and the girls were able to squeeze their slender bodies through the clusters of people as the guard struggled to keep up with their quick pace. The girls made it to the entrance and giggled while they pushed open the heavy glass doors.

"Charity! We did it!" Desiree smiled as she darted across the street towards the bus stop, excited about her new clothes and jewelry. A beefy security officer grabbed Charity's arm to stop her from exiting the mall. She struggled to pull her arm out of his tight grip, panicked, and looked towards her 'partner in crime,' hoping Desiree would look back and come to her rescue. Charity's look of pleading desperation turned to horror as she watched cars screech to a halting stop as Desiree's bag of stolen merchandise flew in the air. As she watched Desiree drop to the hot summer pavement, everything seemed to move in slow motion. Horns blasted, and people screamed as she stood in shock at the scene. Desiree hadn't seen the cars coming in the heat of the moment.

The man holding Charity's arm became distracted by all the commotion and released his grip on her. No longer concerned the guard was monitoring her, Charity slowly walked across the street. Desiree lay on the ground, completely still, with blood slowly seeping from the bottom of her head onto the pavement.

"Is she dead? Oh my God, no! Please, no!"

Sirens blared, and Charity's vision began to blur.

"Hold it right there, Miss!" The security guard grabbed Charity's arm again, yanked her back across the street to the mall property, and handcuffed her in front of the crowd. "You are going to jail, young lady!"

Charity sobbed as she tried to get one last glimpse of her friend before the glass doors to the mall closed behind her. She couldn't see anything from the bodies crowded around Desiree. All she could do was hope and pray her friend pulled through.

The thrill of having new clothes to wear to school was gone. As the guard led Charity to the security office, she felt humiliated. She saw people pointing and smirking at her and heard loud laughter and whispers. Her walk of shame continued past her favorite candy store, and for the first time, the sweet smell of freshly made cotton candy made her sick to her stomach. Not only was she terrified about going to jail, but her heart ached because she was terrified with uncertainty about Desiree.

The guard opened a door with an 'Employees Only' sign at eye level, led Charity to a chair, and ordered her to sit. Charity's eyes scanned the room and saw several security monitors and screens that displayed every corner of the mall. She now understood the slim chance she and Desiree had to get away with their crime.

Within a matter of seconds, a local police officer with eyebrows stuck in a permanent frown entered the room. Charity realized the officer's uniform looked much more official, and they were carrying a gun instead of a flashlight. She swallowed so hard that the guard beside her could hear her gulp.

After the guard and officer exchanged a few words and paperwork, the security guard removed his handcuffs from Charity's hands. The officer walked over to Charity and said, "It's time to go. I will be taking you to the juvenile detention facility from here." He read Charity her rights, squeezed the handcuffs tightly around her wrists, grabbed her arm, and led her on another walk of shame through the mall to his police car.

As Charity entered the front door of the juvenile facility, she was greeted by a stern officer with 'Nathaniel' engraved in her name tag. Nathaniel paused to study Charity's face, smiled, shook her head, and sorted through Charity's belongings.

Officer Nathaniel's face did not show her thoughts, but she saw something in Charity that reminded her of herself when she was younger. She remembered making mistakes that led her to become emotionally stronger and more mature, which eventually fueled her passion for making a difference in the lives of youth within the community. She squinted her eyes and leaned toward Charity's picture ID.

"I see you are from Sunnyvale. Your parents must have money to live in that fancy neighborhood! What's a rich girl like you doing stealing clothes? Can't you just ask your parents for some money? From your address, I'm sure they have plenty of money to spend! While you're at it – ask them if they can give me some too! Ha! Ha! Ha! Now your friend who was with you…is she also from Sunnyvale?" Officer Nathaniel cocked her head away from the ID as she studied Charity's face for a response.

Charity slowly lifted her head and replied with a bewildered tone, "No. She's from Brooksdale."

Nathaniel watched the tears make tracks down Charity's face. Every kid coming in the door the first time was emotionally terrified and scared to death. Every kid reacted with varying emotions – depending upon their background. They could be sobbing from fright or belligerent and argumentative – all deflective actions to handle the strange new experience.

"Oh, I see. She's from the other side of the train tracks. That's a rough area - stealing ain't the way to go to get stuff you need – you ever hear about getting a job? I don't ever want you to end up here again, you hear me? It just don't make no sense to see so many kids with the potential for a bright future here. No sense at all!"

Charity replied, "Yes, ma'am," as her eyes welled with tears. All she could think about was Desiree. Claustrophobia started kicking in when she tried to lift her hands to wipe her tears and struggled with the handcuffs binding her hands. This was just a bitter taste of her new reality.

Officer Nathaniel smiled and said, "Come over here, young lady. We tried to call your parents and can't get ahold of them. We are not able to release you until they come and get you. You can make one phone call, so you better make it count."

Charity's heart thumped in her chest, realizing what would happen once her parents found out where she was. She sighed and picked up the phone to dial the only other number she knew by heart. She heard a few rings then she heard, "Hello?"

Charity paused and replied, "Hey, Honesty, it's me, Charity."

Honesty replied, "Charity? What number are you calling from? Why aren't you home yet? You know mom and dad left me in charge, right? I've been lying to mom and dad to cover for you since I got home from school and found you weren't here, but I'm not going to be able to do this for much longer! Get home now! Oh, my gosh!"

Charity breathed in slowly, "Sis, I'm so sorry... I'm in jail for stealing clothes. I can't come home unless mom and dad come to get me. I know mom and dad are out of town for a few days. This sucks, sis; please don't be mad at me? There's more. Desiree was hit by a car while we were leaving the mall. I don't know if she is alive or dead! Can you please find out where they took her and check on her for me?"

"Suga, your time is up," Officer Nathaniel abruptly cut off the conversation.

Charity began to cry, "Sis, I have to go. Please let mom and dad know where I am, and don't forget Desiree." The phone disconnected.

"I messed up this time. God, please help me," she whispered to herself.

Clink! Clink! Charity snapped out of a daze and looked over at the solid metal door being unlocked with a ring of keys by a skinny female officer with the name 'Adams' engraved on their name tag. Officer Adams had a coldness about her that gave Charity goosebumps.

With authority in her voice, Adams motioned to Charity and bellowed, "Come with me; hurry up!" Officer Adams led Charity to the fingerprint station, rolled Charity's fingerprints on the paper form with the ten fingerprint blocks, and then silently completed some intake forms. After the fingerprinting, Charity looked down at her hands, filled with shame. Her stained hands symbolized how filthy her hands were after today's events. Once Officer Adams completed the forms, she walked over to Charity and pushed her towards the side door which led to the jail cells. "We're going this way."

"Welcome to your new home, girl. Get in there. I don't have all day! Say hello to Brittany." Officer Adams shoved Charity into a cell occupied by a thin, pale-skinned girl with short black hair and tattoos covering her neck and hands.

The girl sat up on the hard cot, frowned, and said, "Something is seriously wrong with that lady…must have 'man problems' or something. I am not here to make friends, so stay out of my way. I'm out of soap, so I will be taking yours." She sarcastically continued, "I see they didn't give you the trendy white jumpsuit I have the privilege to wear. You must not be staying here for too long. Lucky you."

Brittany leaned in, snatched the soap out of Charity's hand, and laid back down on her bed with no remorse.

Shocked, Charity stood there, numb, trying to process what had just happened and why. She had never been treated this way before. She put what was left in her hands down on her bed, checking over her shoulder for Brittany's next move. Brittany rolled over and faced the wall. Charity couldn't tell if Brittany was sleeping or awake and just ignoring her.

Charity finally sat down on her hard bed and scanned her eyes across the tiny cell. The cell had hard, speckly, gray concrete floors, smoky-looking cinderblock walls, a metal sink and toilet, and a tall, narrow window. Her cot was a few steps away from the toilet, reeking of ammonia from a pool of urine around the bottom.

She could hear the voices of other girls screaming at one another through the bars of their cells and the rattle of keys from the guards walking the floors. Charity felt nauseous and yearned to be in her bed with the puffy pillow-top mattress she loved to sink into and the cozy room that smelled like vanilla-scented candles.

Besides being scared out of her mind, all she could think about was a scripture learned years ago in Sunday school. She never really cared to pay attention in class, but one day her Sunday school teacher made her read Deuteronomy 31:6 out loud to the rest of the class. She remembered the scripture and silently repeated it until she eventually fell asleep.

> *"Be strong and courageous. Do not be afraid or terrified because of them, for the Lord your God goes with you; he will never leave nor forsake you."*

"Wake up! It's time to eat."

Startled, Charity woke to Brittany standing over her. She looked around in a panic. Where was she? Why was this bed so hard and lumpy? Who was this tattooed girl in a white jumpsuit? Then reality crashed down on her, and tears welled up in her eyes.

"Tonight we have spaghetti, and I get some of yours and your dessert, so let's go. Consider it tribute for me to protect you here from the others."

Charity stood up. Enough was enough.

"Would you like to ask if I will give you some of my food? You know, that's the proper thing to do."

Brittany responded with a hard shove that pinned Charity against the wall, "Don't have me repeat myself – you don't know who you are messing with."

Charity pushed Brittany back and instantly felt the sting of Brittany's backhand against her face. Charity tried to slap her back - until the wind was knocked out of her when Brittany rammed her knee into Charity's stomach. As Charity slouched over to catch her breath, she turned to see Brittany picking something up to hit her. Realizing this fight was a losing battle, Charity began to scream for help until she felt a huge thump on top of her head and fell to the floor. Then, everything went black.

Charity woke up to a nurse examining her in the medical clinic. As her eyes regained focus, she saw two silhouettes that looked like her mother and father in the background.

"Mom? Dad? Is that you?"

She rubbed her eyes and tried to regain her focus.

Her mom replied, "Yes, Charity, it's us. We got here as soon as possible after your sister told us you were here."

Charity's mom paused and looked at her for a moment, "My goodness, Charity, how many times did that girl hit you?"

The nurse explained Charity's condition to her parents. "She has a concussion from the blow she took to her head and a black eye from the fall. I'm sorry that Charity's cellmate has a history of violence. I'm not too surprised that this happened, and I am not sure why Charity was placed in the cell with her in the first place. Charity's offense was non-violent, and they usually place people in cells with similar offenses around here. We have been pretty crowded around here lately, however."

Officer Adams led Charity and her family toward the front office for discharge. While walking, the other juvenile delinquents taunted Charity by banging on their cells, laughing at her injuries, and mocking her for getting beaten up by Brittany.

Charity's mother looked around in shock, clearly disturbed by what was happening, "Let's hurry up and get out of here," as she quickened her steps.

Once they made it to the front desk, Officer Adams handed her parents forms to sign and explained the next steps.

"Your daughter was only held overnight because you two were not available to pick her up. Otherwise, she would have been released yesterday. I'll be her probation officer, and she will be released with a citation as long as you sign here agreeing she will complete 50 hours of community service within six months from today, which will be the last day in February. This informal probation will end on that date if she completes all the hours and stays out of trouble. Any questions?"

The family nodded, thankful for the light punishment, and Charity's father picked up the smooth pen to sign his name on the documents.

"No, Ma'am, we have no questions. Thank you."

As Charity's dad signed his name on the documents, Officer Nathaniel winked at Charity as she passed by and said, "Take care, young lady. I don't want to see you in this place again," while exiting through the front door to head home.

After completing the paperwork, Adams shoved Charity's belongings across the counter. When Charity lifted her purse, she realized it was a lot lighter now the stolen goods were gone. She felt as empty and deflated as her purse, realizing how badly she had screwed things up. She had never been in this kind of trouble before and had no idea her grand plan would turn out so horribly.

Charity and her family pushed open the front door to the sounds of birds chirping. Her dad put his hat on his head, cleared his throat, and declared, "I smell a change in the air. I guess everything happens for a reason."

On the other hand, Charity's mother found it difficult to embrace the positivity her husband was attempting to lighten up the emotionally charged atmosphere. She walked ahead of them, searching through her contacts in her phone in desperation. After coming across a name, her face lit up like she found a hidden treasure, "Girl, you're lucky I still have this lady's number in my phone. How could I have forgotten about her? It's been a while since we've spoken, but I'm going to connect you with Ms. Wisdom."

"Ms. Wisdom is the owner of the Virtuous Community Center that's not too far from here. The center is a non-profit organization that mainly caters to young ladies and encourages them to be virtuous women." Charity's mother paused briefly as she reflected on a conversation she had with Ms. Wisdom years ago about what it means to be a virtuous woman. She proudly shared the knowledge gained during that conversation as she continued to talk through a wide grin. "Virtuous women know their worth, have a firm foundation in faith and love, and embrace their community." After a pleasant trip down memory lane, Charity's mother snapped back to her current reality and her mood abruptly returned to being distressed. She looked at her husband and sternly said "Come on, let's get in the car so we can hurry up and get home."

When Charity's family got home, her mother rushed to her bedroom to call Ms. Wisdom. Bits and pieces of the conversation leaked through her cracked door. Charity stood at the bedroom door, straining to hear the conversation.

Her mother's voice was cheerful as she spoke to Ms. Wisdom. She could tell her mother was smiling when she said, "I can remember when I first started attending the programs at your community center. I was going through a tough time, and the support I received helped get me on track toward becoming the successful lawyer I am today. Sometimes I feel the lifestyle I can provide my kids is handicapping them."

She paused for a moment. "I need your help. Neither of them understands what it means to struggle, the way I did as a child growing up, and maybe the community center will be a good thing for my daughter. I know the love and support you gave me is what Charity needs."

Charity didn't hear Ms. Wisdom's response, but her mother sounded elated, "Thank you so much, Ms. Wisdom, for allowing Charity to complete all of her community service at the center! Your mentoring will help her so much!"

Charity was happy to know her mother still had hope for her. She tried her best to focus on recovering from her experience at the mall and juvenile hall for a few days while waiting for updates about Desiree. Although she would have probably been able to get the information from Desiree's mother, Charity could not muster up the strength to face her just yet. While Charity lay in her bed silently praying for Desiree, Honesty burst open her bedroom door and ran inside.

"Charity, I found out what hospital Desiree was taken to! No one knows her condition, but it's a start!"

It was the first time Honesty had seen her sister smile that week.

Charity sat up and said, "Thanks so much, sis. Now I have to convince mom to take me to go and see her." Her sister's information confirmed Desiree was still alive, which was a huge relief.

Charity ran up the hall to her parent's wide-open bedroom door. She knocked to announce her presence after finding her parents watching the evening news in their bed.

"Mom, can you please take me to see Desiree? I know what hospital she is in now."

Her mother sighed with relief and said, "Of course, I will. Since tomorrow is a Saturday, I can take you in the morning."

Charity excitedly replied, "Thank you!" and ran back down the hall to her room. She was restless for the remainder of the night and woke up with anxious thoughts about how the visit would turn out.

"Come on, Charity; I'm ready to go!" Charity's mother yelled from downstairs.

The weather was overcast and threatening to rain. By the time she got downstairs, her mother was already in the car. She took a moment to catch her breath. Her mom tooted the car horn. Charity was finally going to see Desiree today. Her mind was flooded with worry – would Desiree want to see her? She could feel her stomach clenching. She looked at herself in the mirror to make sure her makeup covered the yellowing remains of her black eye, grabbed her purse, and sped down the stairs.

Charity swallowed. "I have to face this. Let's do this!" she whispered to herself.

Charity's mother still had not talked about what had happened, so the drive was awkwardly silent. Charity hopped out of the car while it was still pulling up to the curb.

"Careful!" Her mother admonished her. "Charity, please don't be too long! I will be here waiting for you, but I need to do some things later. Don't take too long."

Charity ran to the reception area to get directions to Desiree's room. The front desk was staffed by a little old lady who was cheerfully, but painfully slow, at finding the room number. The old lady's head involuntarily wobbled and jerked away from the chart she was looking at, causing her to search the same area repeatedly. The kind old lady rambled for a while as though she had forgotten what she was seeking. Eventually, another staff member interrupted the tense silence and said, "Can I help you two find something?"

Growing impatient, Charity answered, "I'm looking for Desiree Harris' room. Can you please help me find it? The lady quickly glanced at the chart on the desk, wrote down the room number on a piece of paper, and handed it to Charity.

Charity looked around for the elevator and paused as the antiseptic smells of the hospital attacked her nostrils. The knots were roiling in her stomach again, her head began to ache, and her fingers were shaking, but she could not turn away. She had to face this.

The elevator stopped on the fifth floor and opened to clean white walls and polished floors that made a rubbery sound with every step Charity made. Charity saw the room number from the elevator door … 511. She heard the nurses' rubber shoes squeaking as they walked down the hall and the whoosh, beeps, and chirps of monitoring equipment. She smelled antiseptic, leftover lunches on plastic trays in the hallway, and the leftover scent of someone's perfume that had walked by earlier. The hall lighting was moderately low, with the nurse's station a brighter beacon to her right. She almost tripped over a gurney wheel parked haphazardly beside room 511.

This is it. She could hear the beeps from the equipment and the oxygen monitoring machine. She pushed back the curtain, which revealed Desiree laying still on a narrow bed with the covers in disarray. Charity remembered how Desiree looked laying in the street that fateful day.

Desiree's mother had her head on the bed, praying at her daughter's feet. She looked up with tired eyes, "Hi, Charity. I'm glad that you were able to make it. She is in a coma and on life support. She will not be able to respond to you. They don't know if she will be able to make it through. I am trusting in God. That's all I can do. I will leave you two for a moment while I get some coffee."

Charity could not believe what she had heard. Tears flowed down her face while her eyes wandered around the hospital bed, taking in Desiree's condition.

Her arms and legs were in casts, and bandages wrapped around half her face. Dark brown and yellow bruising showed from under the edge of the bandages. Five catheter lines for blood, plasma, heart monitoring, and other tubes led from bags and machines to her body. Desiree's skin was pasty looking and smelled like she hadn't had a bath in weeks.

Charity kneeled beside the bed and cried out. "God, please forgive me! This was all my fault! It was all my idea! Please, God!"

She recalled her conversation with Desiree in her room the morning they went to the mall to steal clothes. Charity could clearly remember the smell of the pancakes her mother was cooking coming from downstairs. She closed her eyes and could once again hear the chirping of the blue jays in the tall tree in front of her family's home and feel the gentle breeze that came through her slightly cracked bedroom window. It was a typical Saturday in her cozy home.

"Charity, you're lucky to have new clothes for the school year. My parents cannot afford to get me anything new." Desiree shrugged. "I'll be wearing the same ole stuff everyone's already seen. You always look so nice when you come to school. I've seen Michael checking you out lately – in fact, all the time – he can't take his eyes off you. I just want to feel pretty and be noticed for once, just like you are." Desiree slowly put her head down and looked at her worn shoes as she shared her thoughts with her best friend.

Charity smiled and replied, "Let's go to the mall and get some new clothes. I will help you – don't worry about a thing – we got this, girl!

Although Desiree was initially reluctant, Charity convinced her they would get away with it and be back home trying on their new clothes and taking selfies to share on their social media sites before dinner.

Beep. Beep. Beep. The sound of the machines that Desiree was hooked up to snapped Charity from the past to the present. Her friend is no longer wearing worn clothes but a thin, ugly, cotton hospital gown – a far cry from the elegant clothes they had tried to steal.

Charity leaned over Desiree, kissed her forehead, and whispered, "I'm so sorry, Desiree. I should have just given you some of my clothes instead of convincing you to steal. I promise you I will be a better person and friend. Please pull through this."

"I want to share a scripture with you that helps me get through hard times. It's Deuteronomy 31:6, which says, 'Be strong and courageous. Do not be afraid or terrified because of them, for the Lord your God goes with you; he will never leave nor forsake you." If you can hear me, please don't forget this scripture. Think of it every time you feel like giving up and are all alone."

As Charity placed her hand in Desiree's, Desiree clenched Charity's finger.

"You do hear me, Desiree? You are going to get through this! I will be praying for you. I love you! I will see you soon!"

With her spirits lifted, Charity walked back outside to her mother, waiting in the car. Charity was looking forward to meeting Ms. Wisdom and helping at the community center. While in the car, her mother informed her the community service would start the following Monday. She felt a change coming, and she began to believe in the scriptures her Sunday school teacher made her learn. Charity's mother dropped her back at home, and she spent the rest of the evening anticipating her first day of giving back to the community.

"Good Morning! Welcome to the Virtuous Community Center! You must be Charity!"

Charity was a little startled at the overwhelming personality in this woman and instantly thought, "There was something exceptional about this lady."

Ms. Wisdom smothered Charity with a huge hug and a warm smile. Ms. Wisdom had fine wrinkles in the corners of her eyes, a dimply smile, and short, curly hair sprinkled with gray. While she looked like she didn't miss a meal, she moved quickly, yet with purpose. Charity could not help but to straighten up and return a big smile in response to Ms. Wisdom's enthusiasm.

Ms. Wisdom's eyes twinkled as she took a moment to study Charity from head to toe and said, "I am delighted you are here. I believe you were *meant* to be here. What better place could someone named Charity be other than a place that is based on giving and love?"

Charity's heart melted instantly. It was as if Ms. Wisdom did not know why Charity was there in the first place. Charity began to wonder if Ms. Wisdom knew the whole story. 'She had to know,' Charity thought. Ms. Wisdom likely knew all about Charity's story and welcomed her to the center anyway.

"Let me give you a tour of this place. I started this center in my early twenties, and I won't give away my age by telling you how long ago that was. I wanted to give back to this community, which means so much to me."

"I believe in serving people just as Jesus did. You see, he was a servant leader. There are a lot of examples of how Jesus was a servant leader in the bible, but one of my favorites is described in John 13:12-17. After reading this scripture, I was shocked to learn that Jesus humbly washed his disciples' feet! After washing the feet of the people he was a leader of, he encouraged them also to serve the people they would one day lead. This scripture taught me that no matter your position or title, you must stay humble and serve others with love and compassion."

"In time, you will learn what that means – if you want. I have deep roots here. I have met so many kind and gifted people, yet they had a few rough patches. So they came here because they were in need. They, in turn, give back continuously because of the impact this place made on their life."

Ms. Wisdom looked to her right and saw a slender lady. Charity followed her gaze and saw a woman she guessed to be in her early 30s.

"Speaking of someone who is giving back … let me introduce you to the leader of our Youth Department! Ms. Perseverance, I'd like for you to meet Charity!"

Ms. Perseverance had a glow about her and glided when she walked like she didn't have a care in the world.

"Nice to meet you, Charity! We were looking forward to meeting you today! If you don't mind coming, I can get you checked in and started with your first assignment."

Ms. Wisdom saw someone come through the door, and before walking towards the front door, Ms. Wisdom turned towards Charity, "Let's complete the tour later. You have plenty of time to get to know this place." She then gave Charity a sweet smile. Charity watched as Ms. Wisdom walked up to what looked to be a homeless person in the reception area and hugged them.

"Charity, I will have you come with me to the back room where we sort clothes donated by the community. I need you to help me inspect the clothes, sort them into different categories and hang them on racks. We give some of these clothes to people who are experiencing financial difficulties in our neighborhood and sell the designer-brand clothes to shoppers, and the money goes to help feed and clothe others.

Ms. Perseverance led Charity down a brightly decorated hall. Charity's pace slowed as she took a close look at the decorations. The wall was painted a bright and cheery blue and covered with pictures of people laughing and Ms. Wisdom sharing love with people throughout the community. The people pictured were of folks dancing with one another to live music played in the auditorium, candid pictures of donating goods to the homeless in the surrounding areas, and even pictures of a slender, young-looking Ms. Wisdom receiving an award from the city Mayor. Charity was impressed and could not believe that Ms. Wisdom would embrace someone like her – especially after all the trouble she had caused. Charity began to feel overwhelmed by guilt and started falling behind even further.

Ms. Perseverance turned around and noticed Charity's face. "Charity, what's wrong? Is everything Ok?"

Charity sighed and replied, "Do you know why I'm here? Is it just a coincidence you have me sort clothes, or is this a form of punishment?"

Ms. Perseverance walked towards Charity, leaned in, and said, "Honey, I never asked why you were here. All that matters to me is you showed up willing to help and nothing else. You will learn that no one is judged here. Everyone falls short of God's glory, sweetie. We all make mistakes. I can find another task for you if you want to do something else. It's not a problem."

Charity lifted her head and dried her tears. "No, Ms. Perseverance, I can handle sorting the clothes."

Charity and Ms. Perseverance entered a warehouse-sized room with piles of clothes. A lot of them were in almost brand-new condition. She could not help but think about Desiree and how she could have benefited from a giving place like this. If only she knew it existed, she knew Desiree would have loved shopping here.

Shortly after the clothes were sorted and hung on racks, Charity heard voices echoing down the hall.

Ms. Perseverance quickly walked into the room, "Charity, you finished right on time! People are here to shop for clothes for school. Now for the fun part!"

People of all ages, genders, and ethnicities filled the room as Ms. Perseverance handed out bags for them to fill with the clothes they shopped.

She walked up to Charity and said, "Hey, if you see something you like, you can take something with you."

Charity was speechless. She walked around and found a lovely purple scarf. Purple was Desiree's favorite color!

"Can I please have this, Ms. Perseverance?"

"Of course, you can! Nice choice, sweetheart," she replied.

Charity placed the scarf in her bag and heard a loud outburst from one of the kids sorting through clothes.

"Mom! These clothes are horrible! You expect me to wear this stuff to school? Why can't we just go to the mall like everyone else?"

Charity began to feel the heat rising up her neck. She had spent all morning sorting the clothes and preparing them for this ungrateful person. Charity looked at Ms. Perseverance, who was still smiling, and thought, 'Why is she still smiling? Doesn't she hear this spoiled brat complaining over here despite all of our hard work?'

Ms. Perseverance saw Charity's facial expression and walked over to her. "Charity, are you ok?"

"No, I am not! I worked so hard, and people here complain about stuff they don't even have to pay for! I was expecting everyone in here would appreciate our efforts!"

Ms. Perseverance replied, "Charity, I need you to understand we are to give without expectation, just like the bible says. Have you ever read Luke 6:35? When you get a chance to read it, I recommend that verse. Once you truly understand what *your* name means, Charity, you will no longer be bothered by people who respond like this when you give. You won't be disappointed because you were not giving with an expectation of anything. You were simply giving out of the kindness of your heart."

Charity was in awe of Ms. Perseverance's response and quickly changed her attitude toward the situation.

"Charity, are you ready to go?"

Charity turned around and saw her mom waving at her in the doorway. She hugged Ms. Perseverance, "Thank you for the scarf! I hope to see you next time," and left with her mother.

Charity's mother was pleased to see that the community center still had the same loving effect it had on her when she visited years ago. Charity spent the entire drive home talking about her time at the center and the things she learned. When they got home, Charity went to her room, hung the scarf she received in her closet, and prepared herself for another eventful day.

She sighed, plopped backward on her bed, and her head slowly sunk into her foam pillow. "Tomorrow will be my first day back at school since all this mess. I'm certain everyone knows what happened and has been talking bad about me. I wonder if people blame me for what happened to Desiree. I don't feel like going back tomorrow." Charity stared at her ceiling while lost in her thoughts until she was ready to go to bed.

"I'm almost ready, Mom!" Charity looks in the mirror at her outfit one last time. "Something is missing. That purple scarf I got the other day will look perfect with this outfit! My friends at school will be so jealous!"

She put the purple scarf around her neck and ran to her mom's car. Charity pulled down the sun visor and looked in the mirror to check her makeup. She remembered she had picked the scarf specifically for Desiree and felt a sinking feeling in her stomach.

'I will just wear it today and then give the scarf to her the next time I see her,' she convinced herself silently.

The car pulled up to the curb at the school, and she stepped out. She walked and looked off, batting her thickly coated eyelashes as everyone watched her walk down her imaginary fashion runway. Throughout the day, she purposely took bathroom breaks in the middle of class so everyone could watch her come and go. People kept asking her where she got the purple scarf, and she smiled, refusing to tell anyone. The attention she got was exciting; she realized it would be hard to hand the scarf over to Desiree. She pressed on with her day, dreading for all the attention she received to be over.

It was 3:45, and the last bell of the day rang. Charity's last class was physical education, and she was rushing to get dressed because her mother would take her to visit Desiree at the hospital. Hurriedly she changed and ran to the parking lot, where she met her mother. When she arrived at the hospital, she grabbed the gift bag she picked out for Desiree's scarf and reached for her neck to finally say goodbye to her new beloved treasure.

"Oh my gosh! Mom! Where is it?"

Her mother replied, "What are you talking about, Charity?"

Charity's eyes were wide open with fear. "Mom, please take me back to school. I think I left the scarf I got for Desiree in the locker room! Please, Mom, I'm begging you!"

Charity's mom drove her back to her school. Anxiously, Charity searched everywhere and could not find the scarf.

"It's gone! I can't believe this! I'm such a bad friend! How could I be so selfish?" Charity looked up and saw a wall mirror and walked over to it. She looked at herself shamefully and said, "Never again, Charity...enough is enough. I do not like the person you have become. I am done with being selfish."

She walked back to her mother's car, got in, and said, "Mom, it's gone. Can we just go home, please? I don't feel like going to the hospital today."

Charity and her mother drove home in silence. When Charity got home, she crawled into her bed and soaked her pillow in tears of pity. After crying for a while, she looked at her wall calendar. She was supposed to return to the community center the next day. She began to feel a glimpse of hope. She was sure her spirit would be energized with inspiration and encouragement from the ladies at the community center.

"Welcome back, Charity!" Ms. Perseverance gravitated towards Charity and greeted her with a hug. "This is for you. We will be busy today, so this will come in handy."

Charity accepted the bag that Ms. Perseverance handed her. She found a smooshed peanut butter and jelly sandwich, an apple, fruit punch, and crackers.

"Charity, today we are going to go into the community to deliver food to people who are in need. You will be in the van with me and my two daughters, Chastity and Purpose."

Charity was expecting the two girls to be at least five or six years old and was shocked to see that one of them was a teenager. Charity's mouth dropped as she watched Chastity and Purpose load bags of food into the van. Most of Charity's teenage friends had mothers much older than Perseverance. Charity tried to do the math in her head and realized that Perseverance had been a teenage mother.

She fumbled with her words and managed to say, "Hello. It's nice to meet you two. Ms. Perseverance is a nice lady. You're lucky to call her mom."

Chastity waved in response to Charity's greeting and checked her phone. Purpose then looked back to make sure no one else was around before she whispered, "I'm glad you are here to help us...my sister is always so distracted. There are a lot of bags here, and we can use some help."

Once the bags were loaded into the van, the

team of four found their seats and started their day of giving food to needy people. Before they drove off, Perseverance asked everyone to join her in prayer. Charity felt her heart soften as she heard Ms. Perseverance and her daughters pray for the city and those in need. Once they finished the heartfelt prayer, Ms. Perseverance turned on the engine and drove towards the busy city.

Ms. Perseverance drove into parts of the city that were neglected and run down. Boarded-up buildings were littered with graffiti, and the van constantly bumped over pothole-filled roads. The people who walked the streets looked worn down with poverty; many had exhaustion-lined faces. The route they took was through shady-looking neighborhoods that Charity's parents would never approve of visiting, which made the experience much more intriguing.

They made their first stop under a highway overpass near a tent city. The people there knew Ms. Perseverance by name and were happy to see her. A line quickly formed on the sidewalk, and the girls handed out the bags to everyone in line. The people in line were clearly in distress. Charity noticed many people in line wore shoes that were falling apart and clothes that were smelly, soiled, and in bad condition. She never saw anyone look in such bad shape on the side of town where she lived. She was terrified when a man with mental issues, talking to himself and gesturing wildly at imaginary foes, approached her for a bag of food. Afraid of what would happen next, she quickly handed him a bag so he could move out of the line.

Charity watched as Purpose and Chastity treated everyone they dealt with kindly, regardless of how foul they smelled or how much they were covered with dirt. The campsite smelled like feces and strong alcohol, but they stayed there until everyone received a bag. Once their job was done, the ladies piled into the van and continued to the next destination. Charity felt her compassion growing, which sparked a newfound love for giving in the community.

Her stomach began to rumble as Charity delivered the final food bag at the last stop. She remembered the smooshed peanut butter and jelly sandwich Ms. Perseverance gave her and realized that a simple meal didn't sound so bad. She could not wait to get back to the van and eat it.

While walking to the van, she was approached by a little girl with two missing teeth in her smile. The little girl looked at her, grinned, and said, "Do you have some money so I can get something from the ice cream truck?"

Charity looked at the child's worn and dirty clothes. Charity said to the little girl, "I don't have any money on me, but I have some food I can give you."

The little girl smiled even bigger and showed pink gums and a few teeth.

Charity thought, 'Something about this girl reminds me of Desiree.'

Charity grabbed the food sack from the van and handed it to the little girl. The girl began to stuff her mouth immediately. Her sincere, 'thank you!' was muffled by the peanut butter and jelly stuck to the roof of her mouth.

Charity started feeling something she had never felt before. She was glad to see this little girl was able to eat. She now understood the true meaning of giving, and it felt good! She waved goodbye and got into the van.

Ms. Perseverance nodded in approval, "Well done, Charity! I knew you had it in you," started the engine, and drove back to the community center to end their day of service. Perseverance and her daughters thanked Charity for her hard work and hugged her goodbye. When the ladies climbed out of the van, Charity saw her mother was already parked outside the building waiting for her.

Charity had a lot to share with her mother on the way home. She described the van, the girls, the homeless in line, and her feelings after giving the young girl with missing teeth her lunch. Her mom nodded and listened, holding back any judgment of her daughter, knowing from her hard-earned wisdom of past experiences that this community work was just what her daughter needed.

As Charity spoke, her mother realized she had failed to teach her daughters about the importance of giving. She was fortunate to have the money to buy them just about anything they wanted. She now understood that Charity's circumstances could have been different if Charity hadn't been raised to be so selfish. She smiled as Charity shared the details of her day and thought back to what her husband had said the day they left the juvenile hall, "Everything happens for a reason."

As she drove past the sign with the large letters spelling out, "Welcome to Sunnyvale," she nodded in respect to her husband's words, grateful for the opportunity to learn from this experience with her daughter.

Bang! Bang! Charity banged on Honesty's bedroom door. "Honesty! Can you hear me out here? Open the door!"

Charity got no response, so she pushed open the door.

"Honesty, what are you doing? What? Why are you wearing my scarf? I've been looking for that!"

Honesty quickly covered her computer screen and shoved the camera under some books.

"Who was that guy you were talking to? He looks old! Honesty, what are you doing?" Charity grilled her sister, curiosity fueling her questions.

Honesty got up and rushed towards the door, "Get out of my room! You better not tell mom what I was doing! I found your scarf in the gym at school. I figured you didn't want it anymore, so I took it. Tyrone says the scarf makes me look like a grown woman when I wear it." Honesty suddenly bit her lip.

Charity, startled, looked at her sister, "Honesty, who is Tyrone?"

Honesty smiled, "That's my boyfriend's name. I met him online. Anyways don't worry about it. Get out of my room!"

Honesty pushed Charity out of her bedroom and slammed the door.

Charity shook her head and went on with her day. 'At least someone is enjoying the scarf.' Charity cared less about materialistic things, so she did not want to fight about them as she would have in the past. 'I guess she can have it.'

She went back to her room and opened the door to her closet. She looked at all her clothes and started snatching them off their hangers.

"I will give everything Desiree admired in my wardrobe to her tomorrow." She giggled at her idea and began creating a pile of fashionable clothes on the floor.

"This will surely wake her up from her coma! Why didn't I think of this before? I can't wait until tomorrow! I'm going to give all of these clothes to her!"

Charity sorted through her clothes until she was exhausted. She eventually fell asleep, anticipating the sun rising and the beginning of a new day.

"Wake up, Charity! You have a phone call!"

Charity rubbed the sleep out of her eyes and grabbed the phone from her sister.

"Oh yeah, before you get on the phone…I don't need the scarf anymore. I found something Tyrone likes even better!"

Honesty tossed the purple scarf on Charity's bed and ran out of the room. Charity watched her sister leave the room and once again thought, 'who is this guy Honesty is talking to?'

She shook her head, put the phone to her ear, and caught someone sobbing uncontrollably.

"Charity. It's me, Desiree's mother. She's gone, Charity! She didn't make it! I can't talk right now. I just wanted to call and tell you. I have to go. I'm sorry."

The phone line went dead.

Charity sat up in disbelief. She looked over at the pile of clothes she was going to give Desiree, and whimpered. Her throat tightened up, and she felt sick. She ran to the bathroom to vomit.

"Why, God? No! Not Desiree!" She cried between her stomach spasms.

Anger came over her, and she yelled, "What was the point of all this charity stuff? Just to not get the one thing I wanted anyways!"

She remembered what Ms. Perseverance said at the community center – about giving without expectation. Slowly realization came over her, and a peace settled on her shoulders while her grief bubbled up in heavy tears and streamed down her cheeks.

Honesty hovered over Charity at the bathroom door.

"Charity, what's going on?"

The bathroom was warm, and the overwhelming smell of vomit made Honesty gag. She covered her nose and walked over to Charity. She had a bad feeling about the phone call that Charity had just received. Charity slowly lifted her head, "Sis, Desiree is gone!"

Honesty was at a loss for words. Suddenly the smell of vomit didn't bother her as much, and she sat on the floor next to the toilet with her hand on Charity's back.

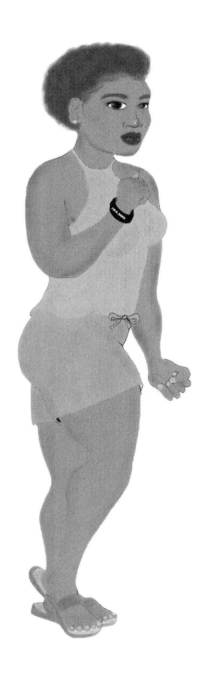

Honesty

"Oh, girl! You have hair that money can't buy! I mean, you look just like me...your beautiful mother. You know my mother didn't name me, Gloria, for nothing. Just take one look at all of this glory!"

Charity laughed as she watched her mother sway her hips, walking across the room. Her mother giggled and continued to brush Charity's hair as she sat adoring her reflection in the mirror of the makeup vanity.

"Girl, that hair of yours is the icing on the cake, I'm telling you! It's full of silky long curls! Your sister, on the other hand – all I have to say is that I'm glad I don't have to pay for you and your sister to get perms. Don't get me wrong. I have the money. I just would rather spend it on something else! I mean, that girl's hair is nappy!"

Honesty could hear her mother and sister in the other room ridiculing the texture of Honesty's hair as she stared at herself in the mirror. Her mother's head was full of smooth wavy hair that fell effortlessly to her shoulders. Honesty looked at herself in the mirror as she pulled the brush through her hair one more time – only to get the bristles caught on yet another kinky curl.

'Why couldn't I look like mom instead of being the ugly duckling in the family? I'll never be as pretty as Charity,' she frowned as she thought to herself. 'At least Tyrone thinks I'm beautiful.'

Thinking of Tyrone, Honesty locked her bedroom door and pulled a hidden box from the back of her closet. She removed a low-cut shirt and makeup she had bought without her mother's knowledge. Once she put the shirt and makeup on, she was confident she no longer looked fourteen years old ... she could swear she looked at least four years older. Tyrone would have no idea that Honesty spent three hours at the mall trying to find the perfect shirt for today's special occasion.

She lied about her age to Tyrone because he might not be interested in dating a 14-year-old since he was twenty-five. After they connected on her favorite dating app, she didn't want to risk pushing him away by telling him the truth about her age. He was so cute and caring. Nothing like the immature boys she interacted with at school. She always felt more mature than the typical 14-year-old in her school.

Although she did not have the best hairstyle, according to her mother, she inherited her mother's full figure, which made her look older. Her grandmother had blamed it on all of the hormones pumped into food nowadays.

Honesty had told Tyrone she was stuck at home with her parents until she figured out what college to attend and that she might get a job instead of college. She continued to fall deeper in love with Tyrone and had what she proudly considered 'adult conversations' behind the locked doors of her bedroom for almost six months.

The dating app they used had filters they could activate to make them look different. Tyrone often made her laugh by turning on the clown or the baby filter. Today he turned on the male' movie star' filter, which made him look like he was about twenty years old. Little stars twinkled around his eyes as he spoke to Honesty.

"Hey, baby…what are you wearing today?" Tyrone smiled as he glanced at Honesty's low-cut shirt through the video chat.

Honesty bashfully replied, "Oh, this old thing? It's just something I threw on."

Today, she was going to do something teachers at school always told her not to do when interacting with people online. She was going to secretly meet with him for the first time. She had dreamed about meeting Tyrone for weeks – how romantic it would be when they first met, and what sweet words he would say to her. She had watched enough movies to know how the first meeting would be – overflowing with romance. Absolutely nothing could go wrong.

"Are you sure that you are ready to do this, Honesty? I can wait for you forever, you know. I really do love you. I want to marry you and make you my wife." Tyrone's deep voice came across sexier than ever. The stars on the dating app seemed to twinkle even brighter around his 'movie star' face.

Honesty lost her breath. She was so ready to become a woman and give him anything he wanted. She had never felt this way before. She knew he was the one she wanted to be with for the rest of her life.

"Yes, Tyrone, I'm ready. I love you, too. I would love to marry you! Just text me the address where you want me to meet you. I'll catch the next bus since my car isn't working now." The lie slipped easily out of her mouth. She was shocked she could keep up the pretense, but the lies to her mom and Tyrone seemed to come so much easier as she dove deeper into her relationship with Tyrone.

Honesty knew she would have sex with her boyfriend for him to stay with her. He's a grown man, and men have needs. Wasn't that what women had to do to keep their men happy? She wasn't going to lose him to someone more willing than she was – although he hadn't mentioned anyone else, she was sure this handsome man had other options. This is the type of stuff she saw happen all the time on the reality TV shows she watched. Besides – he wanted to marry her – so that counted as OK, right?

Everyone else is having sex, so why couldn't she? It didn't seem that big a deal, although her father's sister always preached to her about the importance of saving herself for her future husband. She can remember conversing with her aunt while sitting on her porch at age ten on a hot summer day.

"Honesty, you're blooming into a beautiful young lady. Don't be surprised if those guys chase after you and your good looks. Guard yourself, baby. Everyone ain't got the worth equal to what you have to offer them. You may not understand now, but one day you will."

Honesty admired a picture of her and her aunt hugging in front of a beautifully decorated Christmas tree the year before her aunt died. She wished she could sit on the porch to speak to her aunt again. She then realized it was almost time for her to go and continued to get dressed so she would not miss the bus.

Honesty put on an oversized sweatshirt to cover up her revealing shirt and threw her makeup in her backpack. She sprayed on some of her mother's 'grown woman' perfume.

Before closing the front door, Honesty yelled, "Mom, remember I'm going to Rachel's house after school to study!"

Honesty knew her mother hadn't left for work yet – or she was working another 'work-from-home' day in her home office. Her mother had been paying so much attention to her sister, Charity, lately that when she did not respond to Honesty, that just further justified her plans.

"Whatever! I'm going to be with my man anyways. I don't care!" She paused for another second, listening to see if her mom would answer, but all she heard was her sister preparing her breakfast in the kitchen, clanging the skillet against the stove.

The combination of her parent's ambitious work schedules, and her mother's seeming favoritism towards Charity, left Honesty feeling neglected and looking for attention elsewhere. Her relationship with her dad was good, but he was hardly ever around when her mother mistreated her with emotional judgments about her hair, figure, how she talked, and who she friended in school. Honesty was so tired of the negative comments – and she was pretty sure her mom didn't love her even half as much as her sister. Her mom just tolerated her being around – nothing more.

Honesty held the front door open, silently waiting and hoping her mother would run towards her with a huge embrace. Instead, she heard her mother's work phone ring and knew that call would take priority over her mother, sending her off for the day with a sweet and loving goodbye.

Honesty reflected on a day that she was riding in the car alone with her mother on a sunny day when she was seven years old. The sunroof was open, and the breeze brought a crisp freshness to the air. Honesty remembered looking up at her mother while admiring how beautiful she was. The sun shone perfectly on her golden skin as her wavy hair blew gently around her face. Honesty's mother noticed Honesty staring at her, and when she looked at Honesty, her mom's face clearly showed disgust.

Her mom frowned and said, "Honesty, you look nothing like my family and me. You must have gotten your looks from your dad's side of the family."

Honesty's heart and self-esteem were shattered that day – by her mother and the person she loved and admired. She wondered, what was wrong with getting my looks from my father? Since then, her mother had constantly reminded her she was different looking.

Honesty's dad had attempted to explain why her mother was so big on looks. He explained she was raised in a very divisive household that favored her siblings, who had a 'certain look' to their face, hair, and body types. Sadly, her mother continued the same emotionally abusive behavior towards Honesty and Charity, favoring one daughter and looks over the other.

"Honesty, will you hurry up and close the door? You're going to let bugs in the house!" Honesty's mother yelled up the hall before rushing back to her conference call. Honestly realized her mom hadn't even noticed the first round of makeup she had applied to her face for her meeting with Tyrone.

Honesty sighed and closed the door behind her. She pulled off the oversized sweatshirt at the street corner of her neighborhood and stuffed it in her backpack. She reapplied the hot red lipstick, added more shiny eye shadow, and darkened the black lines around her eyes. Looking at herself in the mirror, she convinced herself that she looked much older with makeup.

"Ok, Honesty, let's do this!" She checked her phone and was delighted to see Tyrone had texted her an address. She paused for a second when she realized the address was in a pretty scary part of town. She didn't want to turn around now. With butterflies in her stomach, she got on the next bus that pulled up and watched her quiet, peaceful neighborhood slowly disappear through the window.

"Excuse me, dear, is anyone sitting here?"

Honesty lifted her head and saw a sweet old face that looked familiar, but she could not remember where she had seen the woman before for some reason.

"No, ma'am, no one is sitting here," Honesty replied with her heart beating fast in her chest and moved over towards the window a little more. She didn't want to talk to anyone. She was anxious about skipping school and meeting her boyfriend in a strange place. Every other seat on the bus was full, and the lady didn't give her much choice.

The lady sat down and looked at her with kind eyes. "Wow, you sure are a pretty young lady. A little less makeup will leave room for that beautiful glow to shine through. And, honey…I don't mean any harm, but I have a sweater you can have. I'd hate to see you catch a cold. The wind is starting to pick up."

Honesty looked down and tried to pull her shirt over her cleavage as high as she could, but it wouldn't budge. "Thanks. I have a sweatshirt. It's in my backpack."

The lady smiled and nodded her head. "So, are you on your way to school? Let me guess, you're in the ninth or tenth grade, right?"

Honesty's eyes widened, and the corners of her mouth dropped. She was sure the makeup and shirt had made her look at least eighteen. That comment was not good news. Tyrone will catch on to her lie once he meets her.

"I'm in the ninth grade, Ma'am, and yes, I am going to school," Honestly reluctantly lied.

"Well, that's good, dear. You know, there is something special about you. You seem to have a purity surrounding yourself. You're not like many other girls I run into on these streets. They seem so broken and lost. They are having sex and honestly don't realize how precious their bodies are to their values and lives. Those poor little girls are having babies, and they are babies themselves. Honey, do you know that your body is the temple of God? Having sex is sinning against your own body when you are not married. If only someone had told me that when I was young and beautiful like you. It's in the book of Corinthians…read your bible…young lady; it will help you figure a lot of things out that I am telling you."

Honesty just sat there with her eyes wide open, thinking, 'Does she know what I'm about to do or something? This is killing the mood for me. Will this lady please just shut up already!'

The bus drifted over to the right side of the road and pulled up to the next stop.

"This is my stop, ma'am. It was nice to meet you."

The old lady smiled, looked Honesty in her eyes, and said, "Stay pure young lady. It was such a joy to meet a young lady like you – you are a rare jewel."

Honesty nodded in polite acceptance and got off the bus with a different feeling than before she got on. She began to question whether she was making the right decision. The doors to the bus closed behind her and left her on the sidewalk, surrounded by homeless people pushing around shopping carts. A few men were standing on the corner staring at her like she was a piece of fresh meat.

One guy yelled out, "Hey, girl! What's your name? You wanna date? I got what you are looking for, baby!"

Honesty started to feel uncomfortable and wished she wore her sweater like the lady on the bus suggested. She acted deaf to the rude man and his suggestions and walked the other way. She felt out of place and scared. Her phone buzzed. It was a text from her sister asking her why she didn't see her at school yet.

This is not how Honesty planned things in her fantasy today. Her phone buzzed again, and reality started to sink in. It was Tyrone.

"Hey, baby! Where are you at, sweetheart? You here?"

Honesty looked around and replied, "I just got off the bus."

She saw a guy walking towards her from the direction she was heading, dressed in baggy jeans and a matching jean jacket, holding a phone to his ear.

"Is that you, girl?" The guy waved, and Honesty's butterflies quickly returned. She returned the wave.

As he approached her, she noticed Tyrone looked older than twenty-five. He also had a funny smell to him when they hugged. A smell similar to the cigarettes some of the kids at her school smoked. As he bent down to tie his worn-down tennis shoes, she noticed a scar on the right side of his face that went from the corner of his eyebrow to the crease in the corner of his lips.

With concern all over her face, Honesty asked, "What happened to your face?"

Tyrone disregarded her question, grabbed her hand, and said, "Come with me, and we can get settled in our hotel room. We can get to know each other a little better." He smiled strangely at her. Not the warm smiles he had shown her on the dating app, but this time the corners of his mouth seemed to exhibit a little smirky undertone.

As they walked, Honesty kept hearing the sweet lady on the bus's voice, *"Keep your purity…. you are a jewel!"*

He only took a few minutes to lead her past the two-story motel lobby, with several unmistakable 'ladies of the night' hanging around the front door. Honesty tried not to stare at them when she realized they also wore dark red lipstick, heavily shadowed eyes, dark eyeliner, low-cut shirts, and high skirts to attract customers. She glanced down at her outfit, embarrassed that she had thought that the outfit was sexy. She felt cheap and trashy now.

Tyrone fumbled with the keys to the motel room door and swung it open, gesturing with his hands for her to enter the room in front of him.

"Here we are, beautiful! It's not much, but it's all I can afford now. Get comfortable and have a seat on the bed."

Tyrone leaned in and kissed her, but the kiss didn't feel like she imagined it would. It was forceful, their teeth bumped, and she felt him bite her lower lip too hard. She touched her lip, glancing at her fingers, and saw a drop of blood. Tyrone didn't smell good, as if he hadn't taken a bath for several days. She couldn't get over how old he looked. He looked as old as her father, and she knew he was at least forty-five years old!

Honesty's phone started to buzz again, and this time she was glad it did.

Tyrone asked, "Who is that? Why don't you just put that phone away and focus on us for now."

Honesty looked at her phone and saw that it was her sister again. Charity's text read, "Honesty, mom just showed up at our school, and everyone is looking for you. Where are you? What's going on?"

Honesty smiled nervously and put the phone in her backpack. She was feeling wrong about Tyrone and this meet-up in person.

Tyrone sat on the squeaky hotel bed next to Honesty, leaned towards her, and said, "I'm starting to think that you were a whole bunch of talk on the phone. You sure are acting funny right now... what's up?"

He reached behind his ear to grab an old cigarette he had tucked away and lit it. The smell of the smoke made Honesty feel nauseous. Although Honesty's body language showed that the smoke bothered her, Tyrone disregarded her signals and continued to enjoy his cigarette in front of her. While exhaling the smoke toward Honesty's face, Tyrone took a long look at her and asked, "How old are you again?"

Honesty looked at Tyrone, her eyes widening, getting ready to panic. After an awkward pause, there was a knock on their hotel door. Tyrone opened the door with a big smile and three guys entered the room.

"Honesty, these are my boys, and they wanted to meet you today."

The men closed the door, and one of the men closed the curtains tight. Honesty felt her stomach drop. The three men looked and smelled like they had slept on the streets. Their eyes were bloodshot, and they were clearly high on drugs.

After observing the strange men, Honesty asked, "Why are they here? I thought it was just going to be you and me?" Honesty stood up from the bed and started to inch towards the bathroom.

"Baby, you said you would do anything to make me happy. I spent money on this room, and you better make it worthwhile!" Tyrone used his soothing persuasive voice on her. His eyes stared her down uncomfortably.

Honesty looked back at Tyrone in horror. He was not the sweet, charming guy he portrayed himself to be. He grabbed her by the arm and threw her on the bed. Honesty realized she was in serious trouble … and no one knew where she was or what was happening to her.

"Oh God, please help me," she silently prayed as her palms began sweating and anxiety kicked at full speed. She started to hyperventilate as she realized she was about to be raped. This was not the way she ever imagined that she would lose her virginity.

"Please, leave me alone! I don't want to do this anymore!" Honesty helplessly looked up at Tyrone with tears in her eyes. He gave her a devilish grin and responded with, "come on, boys, let's make this quick. I'll go first. You can watch."

As Tyrone started to pull off Honesty's skinny jeans forcefully, one of the other guys looked out the window, ducked down, and whispered, "Hey, man, the PoPo is here!"

Tyrone jumped off the bed and peeked out the window in the direction of the activity. A police officer was talking on the radio while walking around the hotel property. Another officer was chatting with one of the women at the front door, and she lifted her hand and pointed straight at the room.

"Hey, man – some chick is pointing to the police where we are! Dude, I'm not going to jail – that girl can't be no more than fifteen years old! Look at her with that makeup! She isn't tricking anyone with that red lipstick!"

Honesty remembered how she was always told the truth would set her free. She screamed, "I'm only 14 years old! You will all go to jail if you touch me!"

All of the men fearfully looked at Tyrone. One guy yelled, "I'm out of here!"

The men started rushing the door, pushing each other to leave the hotel room, including Tyrone, who didn't say a word as he left.

So much for him being her true love. Honesty scrambled off the bed and dropped to her knees, 'Thank you, Lord!' She felt the filthy carpet under her knees, saw the peeling wallpaper, smelled the musty bed covers, and realized she had gotten into a dire predicament. Would she get out of here safely and back on the bus home?

She was still in shock when a loud commotion outside the room, men yelling and shouting, registered in her brain. She mustered up the courage to stand, still shaking and trembling, and walked over to the window. The four men in the motel room were spreadeagled on the ground, surrounded by police officers. She grabbed her backpack, ran outside, and was shocked to see her mother and the lady she had met on the bus behind the police vehicle.

Honesty's mother looked up and burst into tears through her anger.

"Honesty! Get down here right now!"

Honesty did not know her mother had bought a phone package that tracked her and her sister's locations. In the next few minutes, she also learned why the lady on the bus was so familiar. Her mother was trembling and admonishing Honesty, "You better thank God for watching over you today, young lady. You had me so scared all I would find was your dead body! You sat on the bus today next to my friend, Ms. Wisdom. She called me as soon as you got off. You forgot who she was."

Honesty instantly realized why the woman on the bus looked so familiar. She was the lady who ran the non-profit where her sister volunteered for her community service.

Ms. Wisdom walked up to Honesty and said, "It looks like we caught you just in time for you to have your purity still. God is a gracious God, isn't he? He will never leave nor forsake you, and He is always right on time!"

A police officer approached Honesty and said, "Will you step over here, young lady? I have a few questions for you."

Honesty grabbed her sweatshirt from her backpack, pulled it on, and walked to the officer.

"Do you know who you were with today?" he asked.

Honesty replied, "Yes, sir. His name is Tyrone, and the other guys are his friends."

The officer chuckled and asked, "So, he told you his name was Tyrone, huh? His name is Devin, and he is wanted for rape and sex trafficking young ladies just like yourself. Let me guess, you met him online, right?"

Honesty shamefully nodded her head affirmatively.

"Well, young lady, you are fortunate to have people who love you enough to come looking for you. Are you ok? Did they do anything to you?"

Honesty started to cry uncontrollably and responded, "No. You all came right in time. Thank you so much for saving me! I didn't know all of this would happen! I thought he loved me!"

The officer looked at her as his tone softened and turned towards Honesty's mother. "We will charge these four with attempted rape, sexual predation, and conspiring to have sexual relations with a minor, and whatever other charges we can add. I am not sure how hard the charges will stick, but we will work on putting them all in jail for a long time to try to prevent them from victimizing any other young women. I'll give you some resources about keeping your teens safe while they are online. I know Ms. Wisdom has a great program at her center for youth; maybe you can get her more involved. I will update this report and touch base with you about the court dates."

The police officer looked at Honesty, "Be safe, and I will talk to you soon." The officer handed a brochure to Honesty's mother.

Honesty watched the police officers herd the four men into the patrol cars, then drive away.

Ms. Wisdom put her arm around Honesty and led her away from the hotel to her mother's car. "Come on, sweetie, let's get you home so you can get some rest, recover from what might have happened, and then think about what you can do or not do in the future." When they approached the car, Honesty saw the front passenger seat was covered with her mother's laptop and documents for work, so she sat in the back seat with Ms. Wisdom. As she opened the car door, the officer waved goodbye before walking back toward the crime scene. Honesty's mother sat quietly in the driver's seat to catch her breath before driving away.

As the car pulled up into the driveway of their beautiful home, Honesty looked at the entire day with a new perspective. 'This home is really nice...wow. Did it always look this way? I never thought that I would be glad to be home.'

She looked up and saw a piercing blue sky covered with broken clouds. For the first time, she noticed the clouds in the sky weren't as perfect as the pictures in books. Their shapes were inconsistent and jagged, yet the sky was still beautiful. Even more beautiful than what was captured in photos. She looked at her reflection in the window; her eye makeup was smeared with tears, and the dark red lipstick did not fit her age.

She grabbed her sweatshirt bottom and lifted it to wipe off as much makeup as possible. She realized she was no different than the clouds in the sky. Broken, inconsistent at times, jagged around the edges, yet beautiful in her kind of way.

She straightened up in her seat. She was a masterpiece. Despite what her mother said about her, she started to feel encouraged and grateful for a second chance to be her best self.

Honesty's mother hit the brakes at the end of the driveway, slammed the car into park, and glared at Honesty through the rear-view mirror.

"Get your tail upstairs and unplug every electronic device that you have. It's over for you, young lady! Back to the stone age for you!"

Ms. Wisdom softly chuckled and said to Honesty's mom, "Sweetie, do you mind if I had a moment with your daughter?"

"Ms. Wisdom, now ain't the time to talk about Jesus! What she needs is a good butt whooping! I said get your tail out of the car NOW, Honesty!"

Ms. Wisdom slid her business card into Honesty's hand and whispered, "Call me whenever you need someone to talk to 'suga.' Everything is going to be just fine."

"Now, Honesty! And, Ms. Wisdom, I'd appreciate it if you'd wait here while I have a moment with her."

Honesty walked the sidewalk up and through the front door while her mom was hot on her heels. She turned towards her mom once they were in the front hallway.

"Mom, please, I don't need this right now. Today was really hard for me."

"Hard for you! Did you just say that? You have no idea what hard is. Why can't you be just like your sister? At least I always know what she is doing and where she is – not having to second guess where or who she is talking to!"

"Mom, don't you understand that you are why I went looking for love in the first place? You're always talking down on me; I'm never good enough! I just wanted to be accepted, and my family wanted me to be around. I don't get that here! You always tell me how ugly my hair is or I'm not as good as Charity and you!"

Honesty's mother stood staring at her for a few seconds, surprise showing on her face. "That isn't true… you're over-exaggerating. You know what? I've had just about enough of your ungrateful tail. Do us all a favor and leave! Get out! And, leave your phone! You're on your own now. You wanted to be grown so bad – well, have it – good luck and get out of my house!"

Defeated and heartbroken, Honesty held her hand on the front door, hoping her mother would change her mind as she pulled the handle. There was nothing but silence. Honesty's mother stared ahead – refusing to look at Honesty.

"Ok, mom, I will leave. I'm tired of being here anyway."

Ms. Wisdom saw Honesty running back through the front door towards the car and past her down the sidewalk. She was at a loss for words. She gathered her bags and walked towards the front door, which was wide open. The house was neat and decorated with expensive contemporary furniture as far as her eyes could see. She cautiously poked her head through the door and said, "Excuse me, Gloria, it seems like I no longer have any business being here. I'm going to leave now." There was no response.

Ms. Wisdom walked down the driveway, whispering, "And, the cycle continues..."

Scared and clueless, Honesty walked through the neighborhood without knowing where she needed to go. She kept walking until she found a convenience store. She stopped on the sidewalk in front of the store to look through her purse. She searched her wallet and found just enough money to buy a bag of chips and a soda but decided not to spend it.

"I need to make this money count."

She began to wish Tyrone did not get sent to jail for what happened today and thought that maybe he wasn't too bad of an option after all. She could have moved in with him if he wasn't in jail. Feeling desperate, she reached for her lip balm, and Ms. Wisdom's business card fell out of her pocket.

She then remembered the last thing Ms. Wisdom said, "Call me whenever you need someone to talk to 'suga.' Everything is going to be just fine."

While Honesty was tucking her wallet back inside her purse, she saw the front door wing open as someone exited the store. She was excited to see a familiar face - a young lady living a few houses away. Honesty said, "Hey, Melissa! Do you mind if I use your cell phone to make a quick call?"

Melissa quickly shoved a chip in her mouth from a freshly opened bag and handed Honesty her cell phone, "Sure, I got unlimited data anyway."

Honesty dialed the number printed on Ms. Wisdom's business card and held her breath as the phone rang.

Ms. Wisdom answered the phone after the first ring. Almost as if she was anticipating a phone call, "Hello? Hello?"

Honesty paused and said, "Hi, Ms. Wisdom, it's me...Honesty. Do you have a minute to talk?"

Ms. Wisdom replied, "I have all the time you need, sweetie."

Little Virtuosities

Courage

"Come on, everyone, let's hustle, hustle, hustle!" Coach Gates, the school's soccer coach, blew her whistle as Courage knelt to tie her cleats.

Courage loved playing soccer and was always the first pick for the goalkeeper. She gazed around the field, drinking in her surroundings, her peripheral vision enjoying the crispness of the weather and the blue sky overhead. She breathed deeply to pull the pleasant scent of freshly-cut grass in her nostrils to cut through the sharpness of her teammate's sweaty uniforms.

Her teammates called her to catch the ball. She was one of the best on the team at blocking goal shots. She squatted in front of the goal net, digging her cleats firmly into the greenery.

"I can smell victory in the air already," Coach Gates sang in a silly tune with a devilish grin. "Let's get the season started!"

The coach was still pumped after the team made it to the state championships the year before. They were just a few goals away from winning the championships, and she was determined to hang on to her hard-won title this year. The championship games gave Courage's soccer team popularity in her town and built comradery at her school. The camaraderie resulted in larger-than-usual crowds to kick off the season's first practice. The school field and stadium were packed with students and athletes from the boys' soccer and sports teams watching the girls' practice.

Courage settled into her position and dove to block goals while her team cheered her on. It was a hot and humid day outside – the air was so thick Courage felt like she could chew on it like bubble gum – even blowing bubbles with the stickiness of the humidity. Everyone was panting and pulling at their sweaty uniforms, trying to keep them from sticking to their body as they ran up and down the field under the intense sun. As practice progressed, Courage noticed a particularly foul smell after she dove toward the soccer ball.

"What is that smell?" Courage whispered with a frown on her face. She looked around and found no one around her. Standing in front of the goal by herself, she suddenly realized, "Oh, my gosh! Is that me stinking?"

Mrs. Gates blew the whistle, "Good job, everyone! Let's get a head start on getting to the locker room since everyone played pretty hard today. Stop what you're doing, and let's huddle!"

Courage drifted towards the large jug on the sidelines for a drink of water to avoid her teammates and people from the crowd.

"I have to find a way out of here without people smelling me," she thought as she nervously sipped the water.

"You were looking good out there today, Courage!"

Panicking when she heard his voice, Courage turned wide eyes towards her secret crush, David. She looked down and pretended not to hear him as she moved toward the team's huddle. She almost tripped when one of David's friends yelled, "Whew! She smells like a farm animal! Man, that's gross!"

All eyes were now on Courage, and there was no escape. This was a perfect opportunity for Tina, secretly jealous of Courage, to chime in.

"Hey, Courage, you never told us you lived on a farm! Did you roll around in the pig pen before you came to school today, or did you play with your pet skunk?"

The kids on the soccer field erupted in laughter. Courage looked up, shocked that even some of her close friends were laughing. Tina belched out maniacal pig snorts while pointing at Tina.

Courage ran straight to the locker room – her eyes overflowing with tears. In the distance, she could hear Mrs. Gates blowing her whistle, attempting to silence a soccer field full of thunderous laughter.

Courage made it to the locker room door and stood in front of the metal doors, panting. It was difficult for her to catch her breath, so she kneeled with her hands on her knees so she wouldn't fall over. All she wanted to do was to quickly grab her street clothes and leave before the rest of her teammates arrived. She wiped the tears flowing down her cheeks and walked into the girl's locker room.

As she walked to her locker, she overheard someone talking in whispers. She recognized two sisters from around the school campus. She peeped around the corner and saw Charity, the most popular sister of the two, who recently suffered the tragedy of losing her best friend, Desiree, after she was hit by a car. Rumor was they were shoplifting even though Charity's parents were loaded with money.

Courage thought, "Why didn't Charity just give Desiree some of her clothes? She's always wearing the latest trends. I'm sure she had more than enough to spare."

On the other hand, Charity's sister, Honesty, wasn't as popular and appeared to live in Charity's shadow. Knowing about the gossip around the two sisters, Courage strained her ears towards the sisters' conversation, curious to hear about what they were so secretly and seriously talking.

"Honesty, I brought you some clothes. Mom doesn't know I'm doing this. She'd kill me if she found out. She is still mad at you – but won't talk to anyone about kicking you out of the house. Are you doing okay? I'm so sorry. Where are you sleeping?"

Courage was shocked to hear Honesty was homeless. She wondered if anyone else knew this but decided she wouldn't ask or tell anyone about the conversation. She, of all people, knew what it felt like to have people gossiping about your living circumstances. Other students in the school were homeless, and some of their peers looked down on them with an attitude that sometimes bordered on cruelty.

Honesty smiled and reassured her sister, "Charity, don't worry about me. Ms. Wisdom's shelter for women provides a bed and two meals a day. I've been able to volunteer at the Virtuous Community Center to pay my way, and I am taking a few of Ms. Perseverance's' classes about building self-esteem. I'm even helping her with her teen parenting class, which has me reconsidering having any kids of my own any time soon. Having a baby isn't as easy as I thought it would be. Ms. Perseverance cares about the girls and women in her classes. I feel like she has shown me a lot of love. I feel seen for the first time, like I am important, and it feels good."

She added, "Ms. Perseverance said you used to help her with the clothing program, and she misses you, by the way."

Honesty took a moment to look at some of the clothes that Charity gave her and got excited. "Wow, Charity – did you mean to bring me this shirt? This is one of your favorites!"

Charity looked at Honesty with a look of sadness mixed with a little bit of newly found wisdom, "Material things aren't as important to me as they used to be, sis. If you need anything, please let me know, and I will do everything I can to get it to you."

Courage interrupted their conversation by yanking on the heavy lock that kept her belongings securely tucked in her locker. The metallic rattle startled the two sisters to a moment of silence. After realizing someone else was in the locker room, the two sisters hugged and went their separate ways.

"I guess I'm not the only one with issues right now," Courage whispered. She grabbed her clothing out of the locker.

When she leaned over to remove her cleats, she heard the metal doors that led to the practice field scream open on rusty hinges, the doors banging against the wall as the girls crowded into the women's locker room. She could hear Tina giggling and talking about her.

"Maybe Courage will drop off the team and work on her farm full-time after today. I mean, it's about time I get a shot at being the goalkeeper. I can't believe Mrs. Gates chose some first-year student over me for the position! She's not even all that. I mean, she can't even keep up with her hygiene. I mean, we all are sweating out on that field, but whew, she is nasty! Do you know what I mean? You would have thought she hadn't had a shower in a week! Did you smell her? What a loser. Check out this post I just put up about her so everyone can know the truth about our so-called team champion."

A group of girls from the soccer team gathered around Tina's phone to see a picture of Courage blocking a soccer ball from the goal, with noticeable brown streaks under her soccer uniform's underarms and a cartoon graphic of a nearby bed of flowers dying from the horrific smell. The girls laughed hysterically as they passed Tina's phone around to look at her post, already beginning to circulate throughout social media to the school student body.

Courage was shocked and dumbfounded! She began to reflect on the hours she spent with Tina trying to help her do a bicycle kick after practice – when no one else was around. Although Tina was never able to master the skill of the bicycle kick, which consists of kicking the ball in midair while doing a back flip, Courage continued to offer her support. She even kept Tina's request for help a secret, as promised. Courage had considered Tina as a friend. Courage had never betrayed her trust and sincerely hoped for Tina's success on the soccer team.

After a few attempts at unsuccessfully helping Tina learn the bicycle kick, Courage noticed a distance in their friendship but didn't overthink it. Tina began to make jokes about Courage in front of their teammates that increasingly became crueler, but today was the worst it had ever been. Courage listened as Tina continued talking trash about her. Courage felt her stomach twist as she realized Tina was not the friend she had imagined.

As her teammates continued to laugh and gossip, Courage quietly gathered her things and slipped out the side door. While on the bus going home, Courage kept replaying the scenes over the last months with her interactions with Tina.

She couldn't figure out what she could have possibly done to Tina to deserve the scorn, mocking, and cruel treatment. Was it jealousy of the coveted spot on the team or something deeper?

"Courage, is that you? How was your day?" her mom called out as she entered the front door.

Courage quietly closed the door behind her and dropped her bags as she hopelessly stared at her mother while the chilling feeling of defeat emotionally hit her. Her mother calmly gazed at Courage, her eyes wide, dramatically emphasizing the worry lines in the corners of her face.

"What's wrong with you, baby? Did something go wrong at your practice? Did you get kicked off the team? What happened?" Courage's mother rapid-fired questions while shuffling in her house shoes down the hallway to embrace her daughter with a hug.

"Oh, dear! Honey, I think puberty kicked in for you; you got a little overwhelming body odor going on there!"

Courage couldn't take it anymore. She howled and ran up the stairs to the bathroom.

Her mother yelled out, "Did I say something wrong? Don't worry. I will go to the store to pick up some deodorant for you. It's an easy fix. Just shower, and I will be back in a few minutes!"

Minutes later, the floor and walls rattled as the heavy garage door opened and closed below her bedroom wall. Her mother must have gone to the store as she promised.

Courage locked herself in the bathroom and turned up the shower to drown out the noises in her head. Her tears left streaks in patches of dirt that clung to her face during the hard practice in the field. Her dirty face emphasized this worst experience of her life.

She began to imagine her classmates at her school pointing and laughing at her. The gossip and laughter still pummeled her brain as she went through her supposed list of friends who had laughed at her today. All she could hear was the entire soccer field full of kids from her school laughing at her, the circling faces and jeering drowning her thoughts in her head.

Her fantasies about her first kiss with David were shattered. She dreaded seeing his face again. All she could imagine was him laughing at her like everyone else. Her chest felt tight and painful as she looked in the mirror to see puffy eyes looking back at her, revealing an ocean of pain.

Courage's mind continued to race with thoughts about the post that Tina was circulating on social media that would most likely go viral. The toxic emotions and thoughts overwhelmingly bombarded Courage's mind. She covered her ears with trembling hands, "Stop! Stop! Stop!" she begged her mind.

Courage had never understood why people would even consider suicide – until now. She felt alone, like she'd never belong, and there was no way her life could get better. She knew her mother would never understand and would still make her go back to school tomorrow anyway.

She would eventually run into David, who she envisioned would no longer greet her in a flirtatious way but would make animal noises as she walked past him along with his obnoxious friends.

What's the point? She was a laughingstock now. There was no coming back from the past to a hopeful future. Nothing anyone could say or do now would ease her pain. She just needed the pain to end!

She watched her slender hand reach up to open the medicine cabinet – as if it were not attached to her body. She looked for a razor – maybe she could crawl in the tub, cut her wrists, and bleed out. At least there would be less of a mess for her mother to clean up.

"Yeah, mom, just pull the drain plug, and your daughter, with all her problems, will go down the drain. Sprinkle some bathtub cleaner, and the tub is all sparkly and new, and you would never even know I killed myself here."

Courage continued to talk to herself, pressing the envelope to convince herself. Her chest tightened, her breathing pace increased, and she slowly looked back at the cabinet's contents. Wrist-cutting was so messy; she loved her mom and didn't want her to see that nasty mess – much less have to clean it up.

Her eyes focused on the leftover pills prescribed to her mother after a recent surgery. Courage's lips began to tingle, and her head felt hot as she contemplated a quick and cleaner death as she gazed at the pills, focusing on the dosage instructions.

> *'Take one pill every four hours for pain; do not exceed four pills in twenty-four hours. If an accidental overdose, seek medical help immediately, including calling poison control for treatment.'*

A creepy voice whispered, "Do it!" in her ear.

She looked behind her, fully expecting someone to be there. "It's not going to get better, no matter what I do," she whispered.

The creepy voice repeated itself.

"This is the only way out of all of this pain." She explained to her mirror image. She imagined the looks on everyone's faces at her funeral as she took one pill, then a second pill, then a third. Each pill that touched her tongue matched the face of someone who had taunted her, laughed at her, or turned away from what she thought was a true and deep friendship. The looks of 'fake' sadness on their faces, the shock of 'what they had done to her' made her take the pills faster and faster until the water with each pill made her stomach feel waterlogged. When she looked down, the bottle was empty.

She stood looking at herself in the mirror for a long time, watching her image melt, the shadows creeping in and distorting her eyes, her nose, and her body undulating in the rays of sunlight streaming through the window blinds in the dark bathroom.

Then she gasped. "What am I doing? No, No, No, No!"

She twisted herself over the toilet and stuck her finger down her throat. It was too late. The room spun, and she felt like she was falling into a deep hole – spinning, twisting, and falling deeper into the darkness.

"Stay with us, Courage. Please, baby, stay with us!" she heard her mother's voice calling her from a mile away, cajoling her, pleading for Courage to listen.

Courage heard her mother crying and the commotion of bodies hovering around her, and unfamiliar voices. She opened her eyes to find herself lying on her side in a hospital bed, surrounded by medical personnel. She realized there were tubes in her nose and down her throat. The doctor was in the process of pumping warm water down the tube that went from her mouth to her stomach and then siphoning it, so they could remove the pills she had taken.

Courage's mother saw her daughter's eyes open, caught her breath after a deep sob, and cried, "She's awake! My baby is awake!"

The relief was evident on everyone's faces when Courage's eyes darted around the room in a panic. The doctor hovering over her looked at Courage's mom, smiled, and said, "Hold on to your faith. She's going to pull through this just fine."

Courage spent the next day at the hospital for recovery and comprehensive psychiatric observation. The stomach-pumping episode was simply awful, and she never wanted to go through that again. Later she would describe the process as, 'Gross beyond belief!"

In the recovery room, Courage's parents didn't talk about what happened. They made every effort not to pester her with questions, especially since they knew a psychiatric evaluation was scheduled before they could take her home. Their eyes were filled with a mixture of sadness, puzzlement, and relief she was still alive.

She knew her parents struggled to determine what went wrong or what they had done wrong. Courage was relieved she didn't have to be at school for that moment. Everything happened so fast. She couldn't believe she actually could *not* be alive right now. A tear rolled down her cheek as she tried to hide the emotional pain. That evening, long after all the treatments, poking and prodding by nurses and doctors, she felt the presence of her mother sitting beside her hospital bed as she slowly drifted off to a tired, but this time, a natural sleep.

"I love you, too, mom. Thanks for being here," Courage thought as the darkness gently hugged her. "I'm sorry I was so much trouble today."

A nurse woke Courage the next morning when the food tray rattled on the bedside table. Courage could hear cheerful hospital staff exchanging 'good mornings,' and someone whistling a happy tune down the hall. The curtains in her room blew as the air conditioning unit kicked in, which drowned voices from the news reporter providing traffic updates on the TV in her room.

The nurse noticed Courage was awake, "Good morning, Courage. The doctor recommended you eat something light. This is the best I could order from the kitchen for you. Don't worry; you'll be able to eat something more enjoyable soon."

Courage reluctantly sat up to peek at what was on the food tray. She now understood why the nurse was inclined to provide a disclaimer in advance. The breakfast was a cup of water and chicken broth to sip on.

The nurse took Courage's vitals, humming a happy tune, looking at her watch as she counted the pulse beats, and then entered the data in the computer. As she left, she patted Courage on the hand, "Eat up!"

Courage was feeling relatively weak and not in the mood to eat but was happy to see her mother sleeping in a chair beside the bed. The on-call doctor, Dr. Wells, walked into the room with her head down, studying paperwork on a clipboard.

Dr. Wells noticed Courage's mother was sleeping and whispered, "Good morning, how are you feeling?"

Courage replied with a faint croak, "I'm OK," while clearing her sore throat, which still felt rough after the medical staff had removed the tubes.

Dr. Wells paused when she saw Courage's mother slowly sit up in the uncomfortable chair.

"I'm glad to see you both are up and awake! I'm sure you are both looking forward to going home. Courage is recovering nicely, so I can discharge her today. First, we have a psychiatrist that will come in shortly to complete an evaluation and provide any recommendations they may have. Do you have any questions for me?"

Before anyone could say anything, a staff psychiatrist entered the room. Courage's mother stood up to gather her things and said, "I'll let you two have your discussion while I grab something to eat from the cafeteria and check on your father." She then left the room, and Dr. Wells exited the room right behind her.

The psychiatrist waited until the door was completely closed before he said anything. Once the door was shut, he turned to Courage with a tight-lipped grin.

"Hello, Courage, my name is Dr. Jeffery, and I'll be your psychiatrist for the day. I'm sure you are exhausted, but we need to take some time to figure out what's going on with you to give you the right kind of help."

Courage noticed she was beginning to regain her appetite and reached for her chicken broth. She took two big sips of the lukewarm broth to refresh her cotton-dry mouth.

Dr. Jeffery pulled a chair up close to Courage's bed and sat down. He placed all his paperwork on the side table and leaned toward her.

"Courage. Let's have a real conversation about you. Tell me, what's going on? I hear you have so much going for you at school and on your soccer team. Is everything at home okay?"

Courage nodded, "Yes, my parents are great and are not the problem. To be honest, they are one reason I'm glad I am still alive. I know they love me, and it would have broken their hearts. It's hard to even look at them after what I did."

Dr. Jeffery silently took a deep breath, realizing this conversation was going to be a productive one. Courage was coming out of her shell. Courage buried her face in her hands as she began to sob uncontrollably. Dr. Jeffery gave her a moment to release her pain before he could ask any more questions.

Courage continued to talk. "I don't want to die. I just want the pain to go away. It was just too much for me, and I didn't know how to end it all quickly. I'm so sorry. I'm so sorry about all of this."

Dr. Jeffery nodded, acknowledging Courage's feelings, and reassured her. What she had to say mattered. Courage continued to share with him the true problem – the bullying from Tina that had seemed to blow up in massive proportions.

"Courage, I believe this was a minor 'blip' in your life, and your mind was just not working 'normally' due to the stress of school, the sport you were playing, the demand to excel, and peer pressure. Unfortunately, teenagers can be cruel and nasty. I am sure after reflecting on the situation, while you were embarrassed, and there were lots of people that witnessed your embarrassment, I'd bet a hundred dollars many of them would be mortified if they were in your shoes. They could definitely empathize with what you were feeling. But the point is – this passes – it becomes an uncomfortable memory, but – you will survive, move on, and develop better and more pleasant memories."

"I feel, after this conversation, you head towards a better place, mentally. I don't feel you have any wish to revisit the suicide intention. I will recommend you be discharged and have a few counseling sessions with someone who can talk you through some of the issues with which you are struggling. There are patient advocates I can recommend and set up a meeting with before you leave. Does that sound like something to which you would be open?" Dr. Jeffrey seemed to have all the right answers for Courage.

She nodded and smiled. Thank goodness someone understood what she was feeling!

After the evaluation, the psychiatrist excused himself to place a call to a patient advocate and recommended they could have a meet and greet before Courage was discharged from the hospital.

After Dr. Jeffery left, for the first time since Courage was admitted to the hospital, she was alone. She lay in her hospital bed, watching her blanket rise and fall with every breath she took – realizing just how blessed she was to still be alive after what happened.

Overwhelmed with the reality she could have been dead, she sobbed weakly. She held her breath in mid-sob when she heard her parent's voices as they approached the door to her room. She used her blanket to wipe her face and greeted her parents with a wave.

Her parents felt the shift in the atmosphere and her emotions towards a more positive mental attitude. By the look of relief on Courage's face, it was clear the conversation that just took place between her and the psychiatrist had provided a breakthrough. Courage's dad jokingly asked for the TV remote so that they could find something a little less serious than the news to watch while they all waited for the next steps.

An hour later, Dr. Wells gently tapped on the doorsill to Courage's room, "Courage, are you open to a visitor? I want to introduce you to someone." By this time, Courage was getting anxious to leave, and her patience was growing short. Her responses showed she wasn't ready to talk to anyone else.

Dr. Wells gestured to someone in the hallway. A heavy-set woman with short salt-and-pepper hair and kind eyes walked into the room. Courage was confused.

"Who is this lady, and why is she here? I'm not really in the mood to meet anyone else right now. I just want to go home, now, please?"

The doctor put down her clipboard and said, "I understand how you feel, but to get discharged from this hospital, you need to meet with a patient advocate. I'm looking at the psychiatrist's evaluation notes, and it says they mentioned this to you. We outsource our patient advocates. Ms. Wisdom is one of the best in town."

Ms. Wisdom stood by the door and softly said, "I don't mean to intrude; if you'd like, we can talk another time, or if you'd like to work with someone else, I'd completely understand. What you need comes first."

Courage's mother stood up quickly and interjected, "No, please don't go. They say you're the best, and that's what we want for her. Courage, this is the only way you will be able to come home quickly. Please speak with her."

There was a pause as Courage's parents, the doctor, and Ms. Wisdom all looked at Courage expectantly. The doctor looked studiously down at her medical notes, and Ms. Wisdom smiled keenly at Courage.

"We will give you two some space," her mother said and poked Courage's father in the ribs to speed up their departure.

Before Courage could respond, everyone but Ms. Wisdom swiftly left the room.

Courage threw her legs over the side of her hospital bed. She held the back of her hospital gown with one hand to ensure it was secure before shuffling over to the window.

Ms. Wisdom sat in the chair next to Courage's bed and took off her jacket. Courage took a few deep breaths as she looked outside the window, longing to be outside.

After calming down, she turned towards Ms. Wisdom with a blank and emotionally depleted face. She knew this was her last conversation before joining everyone else outside the hospital walls and getting her freedom back. Courage did her best to lighten the mood and speed up her release by reading the words on Ms. Wisdom's shirt aloud.

"Strength and honor are her clothing. Nice shirt. I like that. It's pretty empowering."

Ms. Wisdom smiled and said, "Good! I always keep a few extra shirts for beautiful young ladies like yourself. The quote comes from Proverbs 31:25 and describes a virtuous woman. She's the woman I strive to be every day, but naturally, I fall short of fully becoming exactly like her because no one is perfect. God doesn't expect us to be. The woman described in the Book of Proverbs provides a blueprint for how to live a life of virtue and discusses its benefits. If you are interested, you can take a moment to read it for yourself. That is," Ms. Wisdom paused, "If you have the time in your busy schedule. I heard you have an important goalkeeper position in the soccer team."

Ms. Wisdom reached into her tote bag and pulled out a fuchsia-colored shirt for Courage. "I think this one will fit you just right!"

Courage faintly smiled and replied with a polite,

"Thank you."

Ms. Wisdom looked Courage directly in the eye and said, "Young lady, I'd like to share with you a story about a man named Job in the Bible."

The look on Courage's face showed she had quickly become discouraged again. She realized this conversation would not go as quickly as she thought. Her back stiffened as she rolled her eyes and let out an exhausted, loud sigh, dramatically showing her disinterest in what Ms. Wisdom had to say.

Ms. Wisdom paused again and responded, "I'm sorry; I won't force you to listen to the story if you're not interested. I thought it would help you realize other people have experienced similar situations."

Courage apologized quickly, tears in her eyes, and spoke angrily about her situation.

"I am tired of hearing about or discussing anything that had to do with suicide. I want to go home. I hate wearing this ugly hospital gown and want to eat some real food. I have to figure out how I will go back to school and face my classmates – especially those I thought were friends - who were laughing at me."

A nagging little voice was also telling Courage to be at least polite enough to allow Ms. Wisdom to try to help her. "Go ahead, tell me the story."

Ms. Wisdom studied Courage, seeing her nod in approval to proceed with the story, so she continued.

"Job was a kind, wealthy man who loved his family and adored God. No matter how good of a person he was, his life eventually turned out for the worst. He lost his prized possessions, his children he loved so much died, people talked bad about him, and his body became inflicted with a horrid, painful illness. Job hit rock bottom, and he lost his desire to live. He went so far as to ask God why his mother's pregnancy with him did not end in a miscarriage – preventing his very existence from happening in the first place."

Ms. Wisdom looked at Courage with compassion and said, "I'm not sure what your story is yet, but just like you, Job no longer wanted to live. He still somehow could discover a glimmer of hope despite how bad things were for him."

Courage was no longer pretending to listen but was now interested in finding out where the story was going. She walked over to an empty chair in the room and sat down. She planted her feet on the ground, raised her head, and looked directly into Ms. Wisdom's eyes, waiting for the story to continue.

Ms. Wisdom continued, "Job reached out for help through prayer and seeking counsel. He received the encouragement he needed from a few people who cared enough to be there for him and to help him get through this tough time in his life. Job was able to conquer those thoughts and turn his life around. I am sure it wasn't an easy task. All those burdens were pretty heavy, and he had to work through each of them. He had to muster up his strength despite his misery and defeat to keep pressing on."

"I believe that you will, too. Just give yourself a chance. Like Job, you have people who care about you and see much promise in you. We all need a little extra love and support now and then. It's perfectly ok to ask for help." Ms. Wisdom's voice began to crack as she poured her heart into every word she said to Courage.

While Ms. Wisdom spoke, her face seemed to glow and was illuminated with love. "I know you are willing to give life another chance despite your circumstances," she continued; her gentle voice and sympathetic understanding struck Courage as honest and sincere.

Courage felt warm tears fall from her face. These tears were different, however. They were tears of relief. Finally, someone understood her pain and suffering.

Courage replied, "Thank you so much, Ms. Wisdom. I needed that."

Ms. Wisdom stood up, handed her a small bible, then gently suggested, "Don't take my word. Read it for yourself. I bookmarked a few places in which you might be interested in reading. I'll be in touch with you once you get your strength back. I'll have you come to my community center, where you will be surrounded by inspiration. You will inspire us. You are overflowing with strength and honor! Call me anytime if you need anything."

Ms. Wisdom picked up her purse and gracefully walked out of the room. The atmosphere in the room shifted, and Courage felt a small glimmer of hope. She opened the bible Ms. Wisdom had bookmarked at Proverbs 31:25 and was surprised to see that the entire scripture stated,

> *"Her clothes are strength and honor.*
> *She is full of joy about the future."*

Courage wiped more tears from her eyes, feeling a little unwelcome drumbeat of negativity beating at the back of her brain, "Why is this woman so joyful about the future? She has never been laughed at by an entire soccer field full of people before."

The door opened, and a nurse came in with a stack of papers. "The doctor wanted me to give you these discharge papers. It's time for you to go home now."

Courage knew going home meant returning to the reality she had been trying to escape. Her parents gathered her and her paperwork and other belongings and walked with her down to the car to drive home. When Courage arrived home, she went upstairs – emotionally and mentally drained.

"Why did I do such a stupid thing? What if I never feel like myself again? What if I never can be happy again? What if my friends still hate me and tease me?"

So many ifs, whats, and new questions kept flooding her mind. Again, she could feel that evil voice over her shoulder, whispering negative thoughts. She felt discouraged and plopped down on her bed when she entered her room. She looked up at her parents standing at the door. She smiled a tiny bit as they eased their way into her room and sat on the bed next to her.

Her dad asked, his voice filled with sadness and curiosity, "How are you doing?"

Courage looked up and, in a pain-filled voice, responded, "Honestly, I don't know right now. Do I have to go back to school? I don't want to go back."

Her parents looked at each other, momentarily at a loss for words.

Her mom replied, "Sweetheart, you won't have to face anything alone. Please don't worry about a thing. We are here for you and will support you throughout the next few days, weeks, and months – for the rest of your life. We were heartbroken you thought that…you know…was the only way to relieve your pain. We keep asking ourselves – what did we do wrong?"

Courage stood up and said, "I have to go to the bathroom," and the room became awkwardly silent. When she walked through the door, she noticed a variety of deodorants lined up on the open shelves. She peeked into the medicine cabinet and saw all the prescription medicines were gone.

"How did I become one of those teens you see in those mental health commercials? I thought I was perfectly normal."

Courage's mother knocked on the bathroom door.

"Courage, it's the telephone. It's for you."

Courage opened the door to take the portable house phone from her mother. "Who is it?"

Courage's mother was already halfway down the hallway and didn't respond. Courage picked up the phone to hear a familiar voice.

"Courage, It's Ms. Wisdom. I called to check on you. Do you feel like talking?"

Courage just stood there and didn't respond.

"Well, I'm just reminding you I am here for you, no matter what time of the day. Call me if you need to talk."

Courage took a deep breath and replied, "Actually, I was just deep in thought about things. I'm standing in the bathroom where I took all those pills. I keep trying to figure out what's wrong with me."

Ms. Wisdom replied, "There's nothing wrong with you. It's ok to have mixed feelings. The blessing is you lived to see a new day. Let's focus on what's good right now. Imagine all those negative thoughts as the opposing team. Flex that muscle in your head and deflect those negative thoughts just like you would deflect a soccer ball from scoring as the brilliant goalkeeper you know you are. Remember, love surrounds you, your parents love you, I love you, and God loves you – you are not in this alone."

Courage shrugged, "Yeah, I guess – thanks. Look, I have to go now."

Ms. Wisdom said, "That's fine; I will call and check on you tomorrow unless you need me sooner. You can call me any time of the day or night."

Courage returned to her room to lie down but found her mind racing again. She picked up the shirt Ms. Wisdom gave her and put it on. The shirt was soft with beautiful lettering. Courage felt good when she pulled the shirt over her head. She realized not only did the shirt fit well but so did the quote.

As much as she didn't want to admit it, talking about her feelings out loud felt good. She grabbed her favorite blanket, sunk her head into her pillow, and eventually fell asleep for the remainder of the night. She started to dream about herself as a goalkeeper, kicking the negative thoughts away from her, and then cheering with her teammates as they won the game.

Courage woke up to the sound of her mother pulling back her drapes and letting the sunlight pour into her room.

"Get dressed, Courage. We have somewhere to be in an hour."

"Mom, where are we going?"

She received no response from her mother but got up anyway. She was ready to get outside of the house. Her mother waited until they backed the car out of the garage to tell her where they were going.

"Courage, we are going up to your school right now."

Courage immediately sat up and said, "Stop the car now! I'm not going back there."

Courage's mother sternly replied, "We have a meeting with your coach. If you don't want to stay afterward, you don't have to, I promise."

Courage rolled her eyes and said, "No, stop! What are you doing? I told you I don't want to go back right now!" Courage's mother continued to stare straight ahead. "Fine, whatever!" Courage barked, tears filling her eyes as she stared at the landscape passing by – a familiar route her school bus took daily.

Once the car was parked, Courage's mother looked her in her eyes and said, "You can do this!"

Courage's head was pounding furiously in sync with her heart when her mother pulled into the parking lot of Pleasant Faith High School. She closed her eyes and wondered, "Could I just refuse to move, or will she fuss at me so much that everyone will be staring at me – again?"

The thought of other students staring and laughing at her again prompted her to open the door and walk behind her mom. She knew all eyes and conversations in the hallway would be about her.

There were hardly any students around as they walked through the hallways. She could hear the commotion of students getting settled in their desks to begin their daily lessons. Courage noticed the door to her morning class was pried open, and she could hear the voice of Ms. Jackson, her science teacher, taking roll call.

As she tried to hide beside her mother while they walked by the door, she was startled by a student who was late and speed-walking towards a classroom.

Courage's mother giggled as she saw the young lady trying hard to keep her hair in place while rushing to class. She looked at Courage and whispered, "we know why she was late to class today, don't we?"

Courage blushed and said, "Mom! Shhhh!" Gosh, her mom just knew how to embarrass her. Courage was glad she arrived at school after the morning bell rang, which gave fewer opportunities for her mother to embarrass her. Homelessness As they walked, Courage wondered if everyone knew what had happened to her. She was certain that everyone knew.

After they checked in at the front desk, Courage realized her mom was walking towards the gym offices where Ms. Gates, the soccer coach, had her office. Right before she opened the door to Mrs. Gates' office, she noticed a group of her teammates standing nearby with Tina.

Mrs. Gates greeted Courage with a big hug and said, "Courage, we miss you. We gave Tina a shot at playing the goalkeeper position. Between you and me... it's been a disaster!"

It was the first time Courage had laughed in a long time. The laughter coming from her chest surprised her. It sounded good in her ears.

"So, what do you say, Courage? Are you up for playing in the first game of the season today? If you feel uncomfortable, whenever you are ready to go, you can pack up and leave with no questions asked. I know you are worried about everyone finding out what happened, but that should be the furthest thing from your mind. The students who knew were very sorry about the circumstances. Your true friends are not the ones who will think anything less of you." Coach Gates cocked her head, waiting for Courage's response.

Courage looked at her mom, who nodded in approval. "I packed your uniform and cleats just in case you wanted to try it. I know you will be the biggest advantage this team has to going to the championships again this year."

Courage sat there, trying to process everything in silence. She missed the smell of the grassy field and diving for balls. She missed her teammates. Before she could answer, there was a knock on the door. Courage was surprised to see her dad and Ms. Wisdom walk through the door, lugging her soccer bag, and wearing her high-school logo-emblazoned gear.

How could she resist? Courage lifted her head and said, "Yeah, I'll try it."

Courage put her bag of soccer gear on her shoulder and walked into the girl's locker room, anticipating insults from her teammates. At the end of the school day, just before practice, she was greeted with hugs and cheers.

Her teammates, one by one, stopped by her locker to express how happy they were to see her. Some invited her to sit with them at lunch when she returned to school; others asked if she wanted to grab a burger after the game.

This is not how she envisioned things to be. She was happy, yet still guarded, since she knew she would eventually have to face Tina. Courage did her best to relax a little and got dressed for the game. She was discreetly applying a fresh layer of deodorant just as Tina turned the corner.

"Oh look, Courage is doing us all a favor and putting on some deodorant today! Is that brand strong enough for you? Maybe men's extra strength deodorant would work better against your stench."

Tina let out an evil, crackling laugh and quickly realized she was the only person who found humor in her words. She looked around the locker room, which had suddenly gone deadly quiet as her teammates looked at Tina with disgust.

Everyone on her team knew Courage had attempted suicide because of the bullying, and with no shame, the bully was right back at it.

Instead of joining Tina in laughter, Courage was shocked to hear her teammates stand up for her.

"Tina, you're mad because you aren't playing goalkeeper in today's game!

"Leave her alone!"

"You suck at goalkeeping, and you know it! You should be a better team player and support

Courage!"

"Don't forget how Courage used to help you with your skills after practice, Tina! It's no secret! Why can't you be there for her for once?"

"Tina, stop being so jealous!"

Tina stood gap-mouthed as the admonishments flooded over her. She could not believe how much support Courage was getting. Tina rolled her eyes and shoved her shoulders into a teammate standing by as she angrily stormed around the corner toward her locker to get dressed.

Courage was relieved by the support she was getting and discretely turned away to hide her smile. She knew how she had been affected by Tina's bullying and finally realized how insecure Tina was. Courage saw Tina was intimidated by her, and that's why she was always so mean. Courage decided to take away Tina's power to bully her.

As Courage headed towards the soccer field, she whispered to herself, "Strength and honor are my clothing," and smiled.

When she looked up, she saw David. Before she could look away, he waved and said, "Have a good game today, Courage!"

Suddenly, those fantasies of their first kiss were rekindled, and she was full of joy about the future.

Harmony

"I love you, Lord…and I lift my voice…to worship you…oh, my soul...rejoice," Harmony sang her favorite song while getting dressed for school. It was a freezing winter day, and grandpa could no longer afford to keep the heat running now that grandma was no longer around. She glanced out her window at the ice hanging from the tree branches close to the house.

"Harmony, were you singing that lovely song your grandma always sang? Oh, you sound just like her – my little songbird. For a second, I forgot how cold it was in here. You warmed my heart. Please keep singing."

Harmony's grandpa leaned in the doorway of her bedroom as he took a moment to acknowledge her beautiful voice and embrace the sweet memory of his belated wife. He yearned to go back to those days. He thought he had heard his wife singing while the water was running in the kitchen sink, a morning ritual as she prepared breakfast for the family or washed dishes after every meal. The house never seemed too cold when his wife was around in the winter.

Harmony turned towards her grandpa and said, "Thank you, Paw-Paw. Every time Nana sang this lovely song, my troubles would melt away as each note left her mouth."

It tickled her grandpa that Harmony still called him Paw-Paw after all these years. She had called him that nickname since she was three years old. With all the changes since his wife passed away five years ago, it felt good that some memories remained. Harmony also appreciated the normalcy in her relationship with Paw-Paw. She not only suffered the loss of Nana, but she was still adjusting to living apart from her parents, who had lost guardianship of her after neglect and drug addictions.

Harmony continued to sing as she looked at the time on the old battery-powered clock on her wooden dresser. She would miss her bus to school if she didn't move a little faster. She tried to zip up her coat, but after a few tugs, the zipper broke off and fell on the floor.

"Oh, no! This is the only jacket I have!"

Thinking quickly, she ran to the hallway closet and reached for an ancient sewing kit her grandmother used before she died. Harmony found a safety pin and used it to pin the front of her jacket together.

"This will not work! I have to get out of here, or I'll really be cold if I have to walk to school from here." Since the safety pin did not work, she returned to her room to find another solution.

Harmony layered on two sweaters, a crocheted beanie hat, and her favorite boots. "This will do for now." She nodded her head with satisfaction, grateful her grandmother had the talent, and the love, to have made beanie hats for all her grandchildren as Christmas gifts every year. She rushed out the door to catch her bus.

"Harmony! Aren't you forgetting something?"

Harmony looked backward at the front door to see her frail grandpa, leaning onto the doorsill for balance, holding a lunch bag that barely had anything in it. Harmony knew her Paw-Paw secretly wished he could fill her lunch bag to the rim with an over-stuffed turkey sandwich loaded with mayonnaise, lettuce, and cheese, along with a bag of crunchy chips and the gooey fudge brownies she loved. He did his best to smile while holding the bag toward her. His body was begging for Harmony to hurry up and grab the bag as he shook from the freezing air rushing past the front door.

"Oh, okay, thanks, Paw-Paw!" Harmony grabbed the lunch bag she had intentionally left behind to help the food last long enough until her grandpa received his next monthly check. She had planned to encourage her grandpa to eat it instead of herself.

'We only have two more apples left and almost a week to go. Why does Paw-Paw insist I eat all the food?' she thought. She knew her grandpa loved her and meant well, so she smiled at him with gratitude and put the lunch bag in her backpack.

Harmony ran full speed towards the bus stop. However, the snow covered the ground, and she slipped after running across some slushy snow.

"Great start to this day..." Harmony sarcastically murmured. She finally made it to the street corner and silently screamed while watching her bus moving away from her, kicking up exhaust steam in the cold air. If only she had not gone back to grab that lunch bag, she might not have missed the bus. Now she had to walk to school in the freezing cold without a proper jacket. Harmony shrugged and started singing her favorite song to overcome her frustration. Singing was better than letting the frustration take over.

As she walked, Harmony thought back to that fateful day Nana got the hospital report – that she only had a few more months before the horrible pancreatic cancer would take her life. She remembers Paw-Paw having difficulty getting his key to unlock the front door, and Nana waiting patiently behind him, and rushing up the hallway to open the door. Her grandparents were returning from what should have been just a regular check-up for Nana. Harmony opened the door to find Nana leaning against the stairwell, with wobbly knees, appearing unstable on her feet.

Paw-Paw wasn't beaming with his usual confidence for the first time she could remember. He has always been secure and confident in his every move, but today was different. He seemed lost, fumbling while gathering his keys from the doorstep, and tilting the small bag of groceries, causing bright oranges to spill down the stairs.

Harmony remembered feeling something was terribly wrong. She gathered the oranges that had rolled to the bottom of the front steps. When Harmony returned, she found Nana sitting in the living room, alone, with her face in her hands, sobbing. Harmony shut the front door and set the oranges on the console table before asking her grandma what was wrong.

Her grandma lifted her head, wiped her face dry, and softly explained what the doctor told her and Paw-Paw. Nana then looked out the window towards the sky with glistening eyes. After a few moments of an intense pause, she burst into a song of praise.

Harmony remembers feeling confused. She did not understand why her grandma was singing at such a time and asked, "Why are you singing, Nana? You just got some terrible news. I don't understand."

Harmony's grandma looked at her with tired eyes and said, "Baby, let me share something with you." Nana turned towards the coffee table and picked up her worn bible. Harmony recognized the leather-bound book full of yellow-highlighted scriptures, blue and black notes in the margins, and pieces of paper used as bookmarks. With her hands, she turns to Psalm 34:1-4 and fearlessly read out loud,

"I will bless the Lord at all times;
His praise shall continually be in my

mouth. My soul shall make its boast in the Lord; The humble shall hear of it and be glad. Oh, magnify the Lord with me, and let us exalt His name together. I sought the Lord, and He heard me. And delivered me from all my fears."

Tears slid down Harmony's cheeks as her grandma read the scripture. She realized she had little about to which to feel sad. Her Nana radiated with joy after she finished reading. She simply closed her bible and opened her mouth to release songs of praise which released a burst of joy in the atmosphere that immediately dissipated any trace of sorrow clinging to Harmony's heart. At that moment, nothing else mattered. An incredible cloud of peace and glory filled the room – a moment that Honesty will never forget.

Honk! Honk!
Harmony paused on the sidewalk, her arms crisscrossed in front of her, trying desperately to avoid the cutting, north-eastern wind gusts. She looked over at a van pulling up to the curb. Harmony's grandparents always instructed her not to talk to strangers, but she recognized the name on the side of the van.
"Is everything ok, young lady?" The driver was female with a beauty about her that commanded Harmony's attention. Her eyes were a beautiful shade of brown, her skin glowed with health, and

there was a hint of lipstick on her perfectly plump lips. Harmony scanned the van and saw two high-school-aged girls in the back seat. The lady asked Harmony again, "Do you need a ride? It's terribly cold outside!"

Harmony read the words 'Virtuous Community Center' on the side of the van and realized it was from the community center not too far from where she lived. She also noticed the lady had a shirt on with the community center's logo and let down her guard a little. The lady realized Harmony was uncomfortable, so she stepped out of the van.

"Hi, my name is Perseverance. Wow, isn't it freezing out here? Brrrr. My daughter, Purpose, says you are in her history class. I was dropping her and her sister off at the school now. Want a ride?"

Harmony looked towards the van and saw Purpose waving and smiling.

"Oh yes, I know Purpose! Yes, please, I'd love a ride."

Perseverance looked at Harmony's clothes and saw the broken zipper on her jacket layered over the two sweaters.

"Hold on just a second," and she walked around to open the van's back door. "Harmony, come here and see if this fits you. Our community center recently received a lot of donated jackets, and I think this will be perfect for you. It is used but clean if you don't mind used clothing?" Perseverance looked at Harmony; her eyebrow raised in anticipation of a negative reaction.

Harmony's mouth and eyes shot wide open – she couldn't believe what was happening. This was a blessing in disguise! She hurriedly took off her worn jacket and stuffed it inside her backpack. Perseverance realized Harmony was excited to receive a new coat, regardless of its condition. She reciprocated Harmony's energy as she helped tug the sleeves over her narrow arms.

Harmony climbed into the van and sat next to Purpose.

"Are you ready for today's test, Harmony?"

Harmony had forgotten entirely about her history test today. "Umm... not really. I forgot to study for it – I hope I can just remember everything the teacher lectured in class."

Purpose clenched her teeth together and silently replied, "Me neither."

Perseverance interrupted their conversation with, "I heard that young lady!"

Everyone in the van erupted with laughter, and Harmony felt part of a family for a moment. For the remainder of the trip, everyone enjoyed listening to the music on the radio while driving by snow-covered trees. A song came on that Harmony loved, and she hummed along, then sang the lyrics, not realizing everyone was listening attentively to her. A few seconds after hearing Harmony's voice, a deep, forgotten joy stirred inside Perseverance's soul. She had been tempted to drive the long route to hear Harmony sing a little longer.

Perseverance slapped her thigh with her right hand and said, "Wow, girl, you sure can sing! The community center could use your lovely voice at our upcoming Winter Wonderland Event. Tell your parents, and if you're interested in singing, let me know."

Perseverance looked at Harmony through the van's rearview mirror, flashed a bright smile, and then reached towards the back seat to hand Harmony a flyer with the event details. Harmony leaned forward and took the invitation from Perseverance's hand. The invitation was elegantly wrapped in a sparkly gold envelope, covered with snowflakes and Winter Wonderland in a fancy print, covered in glitter. The invitation itself made Harmony feel like she wouldn't belong there. Harmony's eyebrows quickly went from excitedly raised to downwards and worried.

"Thank you for the invite. I will tell my grandfather and see what he says,' Harmony responded. She then opened her backpack and shoved the invitation behind her old worn jacket, a stark reminder she didn't even have anything nice to wear to such a fancy event. How could she get on stage in front of everyone with anything in her closet? The nice dresses and dress shoes bought by her grandmother years ago were too small for her now.

When they arrived in front of the school, she gathered her belongings, thanked Perseverance for the ride, and opened the van door to the chilly air. As she stepped onto the sidewalk, her shoes seeped into the slushy snow, and her feet felt the burn from the cold. Before Harmony could close the van door, Perseverance yelled, "hold on one moment; I have something for you girls!"

Perseverance reached toward the floor on the passenger's side of the van and grabbed three sacks of food. She then handed one to each of the girls. She and her daughters started their morning preparing an overflow of sack lunches to give to those in need within the community, and she had a few to spare.

"OK, girls, have a blessed day, and good luck on your test!"

Harmony was at a loss for words when she found herself standing with a heavy bag in her hands when the van pulled away. She was excited for the lunch bell to ring for the first time in months. Harmony and Purpose then walked towards the school campus together, laughing and getting to know each other better.

Purpose looked at Harmony's jacket and said, "Now I know where my mom got my jacket! Look! We're twins!" Harmony and Purpose looked at their identical jackets and began to laugh uncontrollably, which drew stares from other kids walking past them on campus.

Purpose caught her breath and unashamedly screamed, "She probably got my whole outfit from the back of that van!" and continued to laugh hysterically. It was refreshing for Harmony to see that Purpose did not care her clothes were used. After a few more belly laughs, Purpose looked down at the red leather-strapped watch on her wrist and said, "We better hurry up before the bell rings and we are late! My Spanish teacher loves handing out detention slips for any reason!

"I'll see you in history class, Harmony...talk to you later!"

Harmony smiled, waved, and took a moment to get a quick snack from the lunch bag weighing down her backpack. As she snacked on some cookies from her lunch bag, she thought, 'I think I have found a new friend!' She sighed, 'I'd never be able to invite her to my house with no food or heat – we will have to hang out at school for now.'

As Harmony stuffed her mouth with the last cookie, she saw her secret crush, Charles, a cute and very popular guy in her art class. As he briskly walked past her, he looked Harmony in her eyes and said, "Hey, Harmony!"

Harmony felt her heart leap in her chest and replied with a mouth full of crushed cookies, "Hey!" Cookie crumbs fell from her mouth and rolled down her new jacket. She was grateful Charles was too much in a rush to notice. She wiped the crumbs off her coat and headed to class blushing behind her bashful smile.

After a long day of school and a dreadful exam, Harmony was glad to be back at home. While she stood on the front porch searching the pockets of her new jacket for her key, she noticed the lights were not on.

'That's strange. Paw-Paw always waits for me to come home from school.' Harmony thought and opened the front door. She found her grandpa relaxing in the living room, and candles lit around the house.

"Is everything ok, Paw-Paw? Why are there candles everywhere? Why won't you just turn the lights on?"

Her grandpa put his head down and said, "Songbird, I couldn't afford the electricity bill. We will have to wait until my social security check comes in next week. At least we have a roof over our heads, right, dear? We will be OK. Don't worry about a thing."

Harmony didn't realize how bad things were until now. Grandma used to handle all the finances and also made extra money selling her famous homemade pies in the community. Without her, grandpa clearly had a hard time keeping things afloat.

Harmony went to the kitchen and opened the sack of food. She was glad she saved some of it to share with her grandpa. She opened the cabinet and found a dusty can of sardines.

"Perfect!" She grabbed some crackers from her bag and put them next to the sardines on a plate. His face lit up with joy when she brought the plate to her grandpa.

After placing the plate of sardines on the coffee table, grandpa responded with a devilish grin, "Now all we need is a little hot sauce!"

Grandpa fanned his hand across the velvety fabric on the side of his comfy recliner until he found the built-in pocket that hid his hot sauce stash. He grabbed a bottle, stood over his plate, and did a two-step dance as he sprinkled it over his sardines. "Now, this is some good eating!"

Harmony and her grandpa sat in the living room eating the cracker and sardine feast next to the candlelight. It was freezing in the house. Harmony could see her warm breath blow from her mouth in the cold air. She was glad to have that moment with her grandpa. Despite her circumstances, she focused on the good in her life, just like her grandmother taught her.

Harmony's grandpa slid his pointing finger across his plate, gathering the remaining residue of his spicy hot sauce mixed with sardine juice and cracker crumbles. He closed his eyes and licked the crumbs from his fingers. He leaned back with a satisfied belly, looked towards Harmony, and noticed her new coat, "Nice coat you have there, Songbird! When did you get that? You are full of surprises today."

Harmony finished washing a cracker down her throat with a glass of water, "Paw-Paw, I know you've always told me not to talk to strangers. Today I met a lady named Perseverance from the Little Virtuosities Community Center." Her grandpa nodded.

"I missed the bus this morning, and she offered me a ride to school so I would not have to walk in the snow. She had some clothes set aside for donations, so she gave me this jacket." Harmony wiggled in her seat with excitement as she continued, "She has a daughter named Purpose, and she goes to my school. She was in the van this morning, too. When we got to school, Purpose noticed she was wearing the same jacket that her mother gave me today."

Harmony chuckled and said, "We laughed so hard when she realized her mother had been giving her clothes from the donation pile; she had no idea until today! I love that it was really not a big deal to her. I think I made a friend today, Paw-Paw!"

Harmony's grandpa leaned back in his recliner, relieved someone was kind enough to do something he wished he could do for Harmony, "I'm very happy for you, Songbird. That jacket looks really nice on you."

They both grinned, taking in the moment.

"Alright, dear, you should start getting ready for bed. You don't want to miss your bus again tomorrow morning."

Harmony stood and kissed her grandpa on the cheek before gathering the plates from the table. Her grandpa grabbed a candle from the table and handed it to Harmony, "This might be helpful when walking down that dark hallway."

Harmony nodded her head and said, "Thank you, Paw-Paw. Have a good night."

Harmony got up early in the morning to do her homework. She couldn't complete her assignments because it was hard to read without any lights, so she had to wait for the sun to rise. The moment the natural light shined through her window, she reluctantly rolled to the right side of her bed, then pulled at her backpack to find the study supplies she needed.

As she pulled schoolbooks out, the flyer Perseverance handed her floated to the floor. Harmony picked up the flyer and realized the event was scheduled for the upcoming Saturday. Harmony thought about the courtesy, diplomatic offer of food, a new coat, and the simple act of kindness that Perseverance showed her. Harmony felt the least she could do was show up and sing. She decided she would do it. She took another look at the flyer to get the details.

"Oh, no! The rehearsal is tonight! I have to tell Paw-Paw."

Harmony found him pouring hot sauce on a fresh plate of Vienna sausages.

"Is something wrong? You look frazzled, Songbird. You know grandma doesn't like it when ..." his voice trailed off when he realized grandma was no longer there to approve or disapprove of Harmony's behavior.

Harmony handed her grandpa the flyer and excitedly said, "Grandpa, I was asked to sing this Saturday at this event."

Paw-Paw's face started to glow as a small smile widened. He had been reminiscing about his wife singing and her beautiful voice. She wasn't too big on showing off her talent to the world, and he was glad to be one of the few people with a front seat

when she sang in the kitchen or the car. He
recognized Harmony was just as humble as her
grandma and was glad someone outside the family
recognized her inherited talent.

"Another thing, rehearsal is tonight. Can I go?"

Her grandpa read the flyer and said, "Oh, how
nice, this is at the Virtuous Community Center. I
know you mentioned this last night, but now that I had
a moment to think about it, that place sounds familiar.
Isn't this the center right up the street?"

Harmony was excited that her grandpa was
supportive of her. "Yes, grandpa! I hope you can
come. I met the lady that's helping put the event
together yesterday. Remember, I told you about her
last night – Perseverance."

Harmony's grandpa hugged her, "I'm proud of
you, songbird. Go for it, and yes, I will be there."

Later in the day, after the conversation with
Paw-Paw, Harmony began to have second thoughts.
She'd never sung in front of an audience before. Was
her voice as good as those around her said? She
began to think, 'What if I mess up and my voice
cracks or something terrible? I'd ruin the whole event.
What was I thinking?'

Her doubts were deflected by reasons she
should sing at the event as she thought about how
excited and supportive her grandpa was. She began
to feel the pressure. If she were to be honest, she
probably would've told Perseverance she couldn't do
it if it weren't for how excited her grandpa was. She

could muster up enough strength to go to her first practice that night after weighing out the pros and cons of her circumstances.

It was a typical noisy Friday on the school bus. While everyone talked about their plans for the weekend, Harmony silently rehearsed the song she was going to sing. She assumed she could perform the way everyone expected after rehearsal the night before. Even if she didn't, at this point, she's convinced herself there was no turning back.

The bus stopped in front of the school, and the students poured out of the bus. Harmony trailed behind the cluster of students while trying to figure out an excuse for why she couldn't perform tomorrow. Just before she reached the crowded front steps of the school, she felt a finger tap her on her shoulder.

"Hi, Harmony! You were amazing at practice yesterday. I'm so glad you decided to be a part of the program. It's going to be a great thing for the community. The ticket sales help the center's goals to help those in need."

It was Perseverance holding a bright red bag. Perseverance had the community center's van park in a no-parking zone along the curb in front of the school with flashing hazard lights. Frustrated parents were trying to get around the van in the jam-packed street, angrily blowing their horns. Slightly embarrassed, Perseverance ducked her head and said, "This is for you. I'm not sure if you already have something to wear tomorrow, but I saw this dress, and I think it will be gorgeous on you. Also, I brought some food from the pantry. There were a lot of donations this week, so I brought you a nice bag of dry foods that you could probably store in your locker until school lets out.

Someone angrily blew their horn, rolled their window, and said, "Will somebody hurry up and move this van out of the way! What kind of idiot would park here!"

Perseverance grinned, waved at the angry driver, then rushed back to the van while shouting over her shoulder, "I better go now. I'll talk to you later!"

Harmony was left feeling more encouraged about singing at the event. She realized she was surrounded by support, and Perseverance meant well. She gladly accepted the food, especially since her grandpa had been struggling to keep food in the house. Singing at the event was the least she could do to express her gratitude.

With her spirits lifted, and her arms full, Harmony rushed to her first class just before the bell rang.

When Harmony entered class, she found an empty seat and draped her dress over it to keep it neat and tidy. She shoved the food bag under her desk as she sat down, eager to get her homework turned in. While fumbling through her stuff, a pencil rolled out of her bag and in front of her worn-down shoes.

Charles, Harmony's crush, leaned over to pick her pencil up for her. She couldn't believe Charles took the time to do that for her, and he didn't mind getting close to her humiliating shoes.

When class was dismissed, Harmony grabbed her dress and the food bag and left the classroom. As she was about to walk through the door, she was met by Charles' bright smile.

"Hey, what's that you're carrying around?"

Harmony looked around to make sure he was talking to her.

"Harmony – are you okay?"

Harmony now knew Charles was talking directly to her and panicked. She responded by freezing in place – starstruck. Out of the corner of her eye, she saw Purpose walking down the hallway.

"Hey, Cuz!" Purpose hugged Charles, distracting him, and turned to Harmony.

"Harmony, I'll see you at the show tomorrow?"

Looking at Charles, she noted as he walked away, "Have a good weekend!"

All Harmony could do was wave.

"Harmony, are you ok?"

Purpose waved her hand in front of Harmony's eyes to break her trance.

"Oh. Yes. I didn't know Charles was your cousin!"

Purpose laughed and said, "Yeah, he's a dork but a nice guy. I can see why all these girls are crazy about him."

Harmony laughed, then said, "I appreciate all your mom has done for me. She gave me this beautiful dress and some food. I'm so thankful to know you and your family."

Purpose gave her a one-armed hug and said, "We are glad to know you, too. I can't wait to hear you sing tomorrow."

Harmony kept a close eye on her new dress and stayed late after school to get help with an assignment from her Spanish teacher. She was able to catch the very last bus home just as it was starting to get dark.

Harmony noticed the porch light was on as she walked up the front sidewalk, showing traces of summer weeds peeking through the snow. Before she could find her key, her grandpa opened the door.

"Harmony, I was worried about you. Why did you get home so late?"

Harmony handed him the bag of food, explained the late Spanish class assistance, and then showed Paw-Paw her new dress.

"It looks like today was full of blessings. My brother surprised me with a visit while you were at school and paid our electric bill when he saw our electricity was off."

Harmony jumped up and down with excitement. "Yes! I can use the curling iron on my hair for tomorrow's event! Thank you, God! Thank you, Uncle David! I thought I would have to wear one of grandma's wigs!"

Harmony and her Grandpa laughed while snacking and putting the food away.

"Good morning, Songbird!"

Harmony woke up to her grandpa standing at the door of her bedroom.

"When you get up, come to the living room. I have something for you."

It felt like Christmas morning. Harmony slipped house shoes on her feet, and she rushed down the hallway to the living room. Harmony's grandpa held a polished wooden box and handed it to her.

"I want you to have this. It was Nana's, and I think it will be perfect for your special debut today."

Harmony opened the box and found a beautiful necklace with a charming songbird attached to a thin but elegant chain.

"It's beautiful, Paw-Paw. Thank you so much." Harmony wiped tears away from her eyes.

"I'm glad you like it, Harmony. I gave this to your grandmother because she reminded me of a songbird every time she sang a song. You, too, have the same gift, and her legacy lives through you. Now I'm giving this to you, my little songbird."

Harmony hugged her grandpa and walked down the chilly hallway to her room to get ready. Thirty minutes later, her hair was neatly pressed with bouncing curls. She found her grandpa lounging in his chair, reading the newspaper.

"Now, aren't you gorgeous!" Her grandpa stood up and strutted around, showing off his three-piece suit in the living room. "I can clean up pretty good for an old guy, can't I?"

Harmony hadn't seen her grandpa with so much energy in a long time and was glad to see this side of him again.

"Yes, sir, you are looking pretty sharp, Paw-Paw!"

Her grandpa opened the front door, gestured as a gentleman would to a lady, and said, "After you!"

As she walked through the door, her grandpa smiled as he noticed she was wearing the necklace he had given her.

When Harmony and her grandpa walked inside the Virtuous Community Center's banquet room, they were greeted with holiday music being played softly on a piano, dimly lit lights, and large, white, cut-out snowflakes hanging from a sparkly ceiling. Each corner of the room had majestic blue lights spotlighting a holiday-themed scene created by the community center's staff and volunteers.

Harmony's eyes followed the blue spotlights to each scene and admired the powdery snowmen, festive human-sized candies, and life-size Christmas carolers. The tables were covered with shiny metallic silver tablecloths and beautiful centerpieces with shimmery white candles glowing against the neatly-placed tableware.

The stage was in the center of the room, with a pianist dressed in a tuxedo and stiff bow tie playing on a white piano. The front of the stage was covered in a soft powdery substance that resembled snow, and a beautifully decorated Christmas tree was just as elegantly decorated as the room in which it was placed. The atmosphere instantly transformed any anxiousness Harmony was feeling into peace.

"Isn't this amazing Paw-Paw?"

He replied with a nod and a smile.

A young lady walked over to them, "Hello, and welcome to our Winter Wonderland event! My name is Honesty, and I'm glad you could make it today. Here are a couple of programs for tonight."

Harmony replied, "Thank you so much! I'll be opening up the event with a song. Remember me at rehearsal?"

Honesty looked at her and said, "I'm so sorry, I didn't recognize you. You look beautiful, by the way! You should probably head backstage before things get started."

Harmony felt nervous again. Her grandpa saw the fear in Harmony's eyes and leaned toward her to kiss her forehead, "You can do this, my little Songbird. I'll be right here cheering for you."

Harmony lifted her head and said, "You're right, Paw-Paw. I can do this!"

Harmony walked towards the hallway, suddenly smelling a wonderful perfume, and heard high heels clicking towards her.

"I'm so glad that you made it, Harmony. Oh, my! You're beautiful!"

Perseverance's pearly white teeth were outlined with smiling, bright red lips.

Something about that compliment made Harmony forget that earlier she had been wearing overly used clothing and worn shoes. She felt like a princess, and a beautiful queen had just acknowledged her beauty. It was her rags-to-riches moment, which was something like a fairytale. She wondered if everything good about the night would turn into a disaster once the clock struck midnight – just like it did in her favorite fairytale.

Just as Harmony embraced her newfound confidence, Charles walked around the corner with Purpose. This time Harmony battled her bashfulness and forced herself to look at his face as he approached her. Charles could truly see her for the first time, and it was his turn to feel nervous.

He stuttered as he said, "Hi, Harmony, you look nice."

Harmony smiled with confident eyes and said, "Thank you."

Perseverance grabbed Harmony's hand, pointed with her other hand towards Ms. Wisdom, and said, "There she is! It's time to head to the stage."

Harmony looked back to say goodbye to her Paw-Paw and noticed him smiling, but not at her. He was looking at Ms. Wisdom. It was a familiar smile similar to when grandma was around.

'That's interesting,' she thought and giggled as she walked away with Perseverance.

Harmony stood backstage, listening to Ms. Wisdom making the opening remarks. The crowd was cheerful, the live band was upbeat with a cool vibe, and the crowd was standing-room-only. This wasn't a typical community center event. It felt like something that would require high-priced tickets for admission. The event was obviously put together with great attention to detail and a lot of love.

"Please join me in welcoming Harmony to the stage! She will bless us with her beautiful voice."

Harmony heard the crowd clapping, and before taking a step, she reached to her neck to touch the necklace her grandpa had given her. She gave the songbird hanging on the chain a kiss, then stepped forward to sing from her heart. As the band played, she swayed to the music. It all felt so natural for her. She sang as though no one else was in the room. The last key was struck on the piano. Harmony lowered the microphone from her face, and the room erupted with the longest applause she's ever heard. She could see her grandpa standing and cheering in the front row next to Perseverance.

For this moment, everything that was not right in her life didn't matter. This was her moment. She was shining. It didn't matter that she wore second-hand clothes, they relied on meals from the food pantry, or they didn't have electricity or heat in their home consistently. It didn't matter that her grades were failing because she didn't have enough light to study after the winter sun set for the day. It didn't matter that her grandfather was wearing his only suit that was thirty years old and shiny from ironing the wrinkles and creases.

Ms. Wisdom walked up to her and gave her an enormous hug, then whispered, "I'm proud of you."

Harmony felt like her grandma was talking to her through Ms. Wisdom's mouth. It had a familiar feeling of genuine love, filling a void in her.

As Harmony walked off the stage, she saw Charles standing there waiting. He bashfully said, "Hi, Harmony." She never saw him pay this much attention to her this way before. He was always so confident and could always approach her while at school. She thought, 'Why is he acting so shy right now? He's the popular one at school, not me.'

"Hi, Charles," Harmony fed off of Charles' nervousness and tried to distract herself by using her hands to push her curly hair away from her face.

Charles mustered up some courage and said, "Um, I wanted to know if we could exchange numbers so we could hang out sometime. Maybe go to the skating rink or something?"

Harmony couldn't believe what she was hearing. For a moment, she forgot she had a beautiful dress and thought she was back in class wearing worn shoes and having a bagged lunch with only an apple.

"You want to hang out with me?"

Purpose, who had been eavesdropping a few feet away, quickly interrupted Harmony's response and said, "I'm sorry for butting in, but yes, she will give you her number, but you better be nice to her, Charles. I actually like her!"

They all laughed, and all the tension instantly went away. Harmony was glad Purpose had saved her from ruining a perfect moment, took a deep breath, and gave Charles her number. Harmony explained to Charles the number she provided was her house phone, but before she could explain she was not in the position to have a cell phone, Purpose interjected again and said, "It doesn't matter what he calls; he'll be glad that he's able to call you girl!"

Charles gently pushed Purpose, and said, "Okay, Cuz, don't you have something else to do around here? Shouldn't you be helping Auntie Perseverance?" as he continued to giggle, relieved Harmony had given him her number.

"Hey, Paw-Paw, I'm going to the skating rink to meet up with some friends," Harmony yelled as she was on her way out the front door. Her grandpa whistled while walking towards the front door, well dressed, with his keys in his hands.

"Sounds good, honey; I hope you have a good time." He handed Harmony some money as he rushed past her to exit the door.

Harmony put the dollar bills in her back pocket, then paused. "You look nice today. Is that cologne I smell? Where are you going?"

Harmony's grandpa chuckled and said, "I'm heading to the community center to help."

Harmony laughed and replied, "With cologne? Since when did you wear cologne to do community service?"

Harmony's grandpa smiled, "There's nothing wrong with trying something new now and then."

Harmony slid out the front door before her grandpa closed it behind him. She saw Ms. Perseverance's van waiting across the street. Charles waved at her through the window as she scanned the van with her eyes. She felt butterflies in her stomach.

After hugging her grandpa goodbye, she looked at him and said, "Yeah, Paw-Paw, you're right. There's nothing wrong with trying something new. Enjoy yourself."

Her grandpa nodded and happily whistled while walking down the street, just like he did when he was younger.

Perseverance

Perseverance smiled as she watched a group of girls with glowing faces and maternity shirts clinging to their various-sized baby bumps. The young ladies were chatting and enjoying healthy refreshments in the Virtuous Community Center's auditorium. She was excited to see her teen parenting class growing. The seats that surrounded seven circular tables were filled.

The attendees enjoyed themselves enough to hang out afterward – even though it was nearly noon on a Saturday morning. Perseverance offered her classes twice a month on Saturdays to accommodate students with busy weekday schedules. The sound of laughter and the smell of hot cocoa simmering in her oversized coffee cup gave her a lovely warm sensation that radiated throughout her body.

"This is pure joy," Perseverance whispered to herself.

"Hi, Ms. Perseverance! I just wanted to thank you for the class today. The discussion was constructive. Who would've known there were so many resources for teen moms? I was so afraid and humiliated when I found out I was pregnant...well, I kind of am still afraid, but more encouraged now. I'm so grateful to have met you. Oh, my mom is here to pick me up. See you next week!"

Maya, a first-time student in the teen parenting class at the Virtuous Community Center, leaned towards Perseverance and smothered her with a hug. Perseverance smiled and waved goodbye to Maya as she waddled like a penguin towards the front door, feeling a deep sense of joy and gratitude for the opportunity to help young ladies thrive, regardless of their circumstances.

Each of these ladies reminded her of when she was young and pregnant. She remembered feeling isolated and unsupported until she took a similar class at the Virtuous Community Center and was glad to offer the same support to others who were feeling just as she did.

Ms. Wisdom walked down the hall, overhearing the conversation, and gently put her hand on Perseverance's shoulder. Perseverance turned towards Ms. Wisdom with tears in her eyes and said, "If she only knew how much I truly understand how she feels."

Ms. Wisdom nodded and said, "I remember you had the same hopeful face after you first attended a class here years ago. She will be okay because you used your experiences to push forward and help others. I'm proud of you."

A visitor swung open the heavy wooden front door, inviting the morning sunlight into the hallway. Ms. Wisdom whispered, "I'll talk to you later," and hurried towards the visitor.

Perseverance walked into her private business office, closed the door, and reminisced about her journey from where she was fifteen years ago to where she was now. She softly chuckled as she thought about a conversation with her childhood friend, Angie, while driving home from shopping at the mall. She pulled out a tiny mirrored compact to check her makeup, drifting off into thought.

"Girl, I can't wait to wear my new outfit tomorrow. All eyes will be on me at the basketball game, for sure. Speaking of the game, Perseverance, did you hear about how cute the new point guard is? I've been hitting squats for the past month to make sure I fit my pants just right - don't be mad if I cost our team a few points if he double-dribbles while his eyes lock in on my booty as I walk to the snack bar!"

Angie bit her bottom lip and threw her hands on the dashboard while gyrating in her seat, showing off her sexy dance moves. She laughed so hard that she started to snort through her nose.

"Angie, stop! I'm trying to drive; you know I just got my license! Stop-being-stupid!"

Perseverance felt a slight bump when the car hit the sloping curb. She yanked the steering wheel back towards her lane as the bottom of her car thumped along the rumble strip on the road.

Angie sits up straight and says, "Oh, I forgot! What's his name got you whipped?"

Perseverance sharply turned towards the passenger's seat and raised her voice, "His name is Daemon, Angie. Stop playing like you don't know. I talk about him all the time."

Angie snippily replies, "Yes, how can I forget? We couldn't even enjoy ourselves at the mall because you were so concerned about returning at what he considered a decent time. Don't you think that's a little too controlling? You are seventeen years old. You *already* have your parents telling you what to do; they don't bug you even half as much as Daemon. Why does Daemon feel like he needs to order you around?"

Perseverance continued to drive in silence. In her heart, she knew Angie was right, but denied the truth, "No, Angie, he just gets worried about me, that's all."

Angie rolled her eyes, snapping back, "That's what you want to call it? Whatever."

Perseverance rolled her eyes back, looked at the clock on her dashboard, and then put more weight on the gas pedal. Once she exited the freeway, she could feel her anxiety smooth out as she glided over the freshly paved ramp that glistened under the night sky. As they turned onto the corner of her neighborhood street, they were greeted by a car screeching towards them with blinding high-beam lights. Perseverance screamed and slammed on the brakes, causing her car to stop in the middle of the street. She was terrified because she knew exactly who it was – Daemon.

Eyes frozen wide, Angie whispers, "Is that Daemon? Oh, my gosh! It is him, isn't it? I knew he was crazy."

Perseverance saw a tall silhouette against the sunset leap out of the other car and stomp towards her car. Daemon yanked on her door handle, causing the door to fly open. "Where you been?"

Perseverance nervously replied, "At the mall with Angie."

Daemon's face seemed to morph into a horrible, frightening ogre as he was overcome with outrage as he caught sight of the bags in the back seat. "You had me waiting around for this junk!"

Daemon opened the door to the backseat of the car, jerked the bags out of the car, and threw them on the ground, kicking and stomping. As Daemon stormed back towards his car, Perseverance quickly jumped out, gathered the bags, threw them back in the car, slammed her door shut, and got back on the road toward Angie's house. She looked towards the passenger's seat to check on her friend and used the little breath left in her to say,

"Are you okay, Angie?"

Angie's eyes were still frozen in shock. She finally broke the silence with a strangled scream.

"Take me home now! How do you deal with that? He's crazy! Perseverance! Aren't you afraid he might hurt you? You need to consider some things and not take this lightly. Please don't get pregnant by him…please!"

Perseverance silently pulled her car into Angie's driveway, "I'm sorry about what happened."

As Angie sorted through the clothes all over the car's back seat, she saw Daemon pull up and park his car across the street from the house.

"Wow, he followed us. Great, now he knows where I live. Girl…I will find another ride to the game tomorrow. I can't go through this again – be safe."

Perseverance rolled down her window and yelled, "Daemon! Why are you following me?"

He replied, "You *my* girl, and I'll do what I want. You messed up tonight; you know that! You better not have been chilling with no other dudes today! Let me find out…"

The porch light to Angie's house turned on, and dogs barked throughout the neighborhood due to all the commotion. A slender, dark-skinned man with a salt and pepper beard, wearing a heavy, plaid housecoat over a tee shirt and leisure pants, walked briskly down the driveway towards Daemon's car.

"Do we have a problem out here, Perseverance? Is this guy messing with you?"

Daemon pointed a menacing 'I see you' finger gesture towards the girls, rolled his window up, sped down the street, and blasted his music, polluting the peaceful air in the neighborhood. Perseverance burst into tears as Angie's dad walked to the car.

"How are you doing, young lady?"

"I'm doing okay, Mr. Peters. Thanks for your help tonight."

There was a long silence as Mr. Peters gathered his thoughts. He studied Perseverance's face, the tears on her cheeks, and the worry lines between her eyes. He noticed the short red dress that clung to her body. Perseverance was a beautiful young lady, and after one look at what she had on, he could see why her boyfriend would be jealous, especially if her boyfriend were insecure.

"Perseverance, you shouldn't be dealing with a young man like that. You deserve better. Does your dad know this is going on?"

Perseverance lowers her head and replies, "My dad hasn't been around lately. After dad left, Daemon stepped to the plate to take care of me. He buys me things," she paused, "He is ... very supportive. I am sure he loves me."

Mr. Peters shook his head, "Young lady, that's not love. Love does not treat you the way you were treated tonight. I'm sorry your dad isn't around. I see you are doing your best to find the love you are not getting from your dad, but I'll say it again...that's not love. Perseverance, you have a lot of promise, and I'd hate to see you throw it all away for someone nasty and controlling like that boy. Wait out here while I get my car keys. Angie and I will follow you home to ensure you get in safely."

Perseverance turned on the engine to her red Mustang and looked in the rear-view mirror. Her makeup-streaked face gazed back at her. This incident made her think about a recent fight with Daemon. The fights were getting worse and more frequent.

'I look like a hot mess. Why would Daemon want to be around me if he saw me now? I have to do better than this. What is it that Mr. Peters sees? What promise is he talking about?' she sighed as her brain performed mental gymnastics with her emotions.

The engine of Mr. Peter's car startled her. She realized she was still jumpy and was relieved her friend's dad would follow her home. She wished her dad was around to do the same. Maybe if he were, she wouldn't be in this abusive relationship.

It took everything in her not to take the longest route possible home. She knew her mother would have something to say to her the moment she walked through the door. She always did, especially since her dad was no longer around. Besides, her mom needed someone on which to take out her frustrations, didn't she?

Sooner than she hoped, Perseverance approached the home her mom was renting, nestled in the center of a line of cookie-cutter, multicolored homes. The house cost more to rent than they could comfortably afford, but it helped keep up the illusion they were doing well for themselves. They dreaded every time the doorbell rang because they were always on the brink of being served an eviction notice.

Perseverance parked her car in her driveway, gathered her bags, and rushed to her front door. She nervously looked up and down the street. When she felt the coast was clear, she waved goodbye to Angie and her dad.

Just as she pushed the house key into the keyhole, her mother abruptly opened the door.

"Why are you just now getting home? This house hasn't been cleaned and don't you have homework to do? Speaking of homework, I haven't seen a report card all semester. What's going on? You know you only have that car because of my two-hour commute, and your dad is no longer around. I would have taken the keys from you long ago otherwise. I better not find out you've missed school to be with your boyfriend!"

Perseverance tried to avoid the question about the report card since she had been secretly taking them from the mailbox to hide her failing grades.

"Answer me, young lady…where's your report card? Shouldn't you have had a few by now? Don't make me call up to the school."

Perseverance avoided looking her mother in the face.

"Mom, I don't know. Maybe they haven't sent them out yet," and rushed to the bathroom to avoid further questions.

Perseverance locked the bathroom door, closed the lid on the toilet, and sat down on top of it. She was finally able to let out the bottled-up tears. Streams of frustration rolled down her cheeks as she thought about her mess of a relationship.

Last summer, she was hanging at a park up the street from Angie's house with a group of friends, and there he was. Brown skin, curly hair, light brown eyes, and an unforgettable smile. Daemon's skin seemed to glisten in the sun as he drove up in an old Camaro in pretty bad shape. The black paint on his car was chipped and faded, his car made a disturbing rumbling noise as he pulled into a parking space, and the driver's mirror was duct-taped on the side of his door.

The quiet chit-chat that Perseverance was having with her friends Angie, Sarah, and Erika were drowned out by the loud music and laughter pouring from Daemon's car, which was packed with four other guys. Despite the condition of his car, Daemon stepped out dressed to impress. He and his friends were headed towards a group at the basketball court when he turned toward the picnic table where Perseverance and her friends were sitting.

She could overhear Daemon telling his friends that he would catch up with them later, and he headed towards the picnic table with his eyes locked in on Perseverance. It was a hot day, so she wore shorts and a tee shirt with the word 'Cutie' printed across the front. Perseverance was mesmerized by Daemon's good looks, and when he approached her, she melted when she smelled his cologne.

It didn't take long for her to fall in love with Daemon. Not only was he good-looking, but he knew all the right things to say to make her smile. He was always around and wanted to spend time with her. Everywhere she went, he wanted to go with her. She thought it was charming at first.

However, as time went on, she wanted more time to spend with her friends or simply be alone, and he would sulk or respond with a nasty tone of voice or complain she didn't love him enough to spend all her time with him. He began to accuse her of wanting to spend time with other guys and began to show up to places unannounced.

On days Perseverance went to school, Daemon would find her and demand they leave and spend some time together. As a result, her grades started slipping. Lately, she had been worried he was following her everywhere she went – to school, the mall, church, or outings with her girlfriends. Today was another example of his suffocating jealousy. His attention had gotten so stifling she began to stop answering his phone calls. Although she feared what he would do later if she didn't answer or return his calls.

Perseverance was startled when her mother banged on the bathroom door. "Perseverance, hurry up and get in that kitchen. Them dishes aint' gonna wash themselves!"

Perseverance flushed the toilet and washed her face at the sink. She held a cold towel over her eyes to help the swelling go down.

Her purse vibrated as she entered her bedroom to place her things on her bed. She had a sinking feeling it was Daemon. She reached into her purse to find ten missed calls from him on her cell phone. She must not have heard it buzzing while crying in the bathroom. She threw her phone on her bed before heading to the kitchen to wash dishes.

She had settled down from the dramatic evening by the time she finished cleaning the dishes. Emotionally drained, she headed to her bedroom, hoping to get some rest. When she opened her bedroom door, she noticed a flashing light indicating missed calls on her phone. The stress she felt earlier swept back over her as she saw that she had five more missed calls from Daemon. She peeked outside her bedroom window to ensure he was not standing there and tugged at the lock to check it was secure. She powered her phone off and crawled into bed. It was hard to sleep worrying about Daemon's response the next day.

Sonya, a student assistant that worked in the school's counseling office, walked into the classroom and handed a note to the teacher. Ms. Raven looked over her glasses, balanced precariously on the tip of her nose, and waved the note and hall pass at Perseverance.

Perseverance looked down, read the note, and thought, 'Why does Mr. Solomon want to see me? I didn't request a career counseling session?'

Perseverance's shoes squeaking down the dingy hallway leading to the counseling office's main door distracted her from worrisome thoughts. She felt her poor attendance and even worse grades were coming to a head.

When she opened the old and worn door, she was greeted with the back of Mr. Solomon's head covered with a thin, slick combover as he searched through a filing cabinet.

"Mr. Solomon, did you want to speak with me?"

Mr. Solomon looked up from the filing cabinet after grabbing a file. He then closed and locked it before walking towards his office. He smiled at her.

"Yes, Perseverance, please follow me into my office."

Perseverance reluctantly sat down in the squeaky chair in front of his desk.

"Your mother called the school today asking about your grades to find out you've been failing all your classes except for physical education. Would you explain why she hasn't received a single progress report? According to our records, we've sent three reports to your house by mail this year, and your mother hasn't received a single one of them."

He paused and received nothing in response but a long, deep stare. The clock on the wall beside her ticked in a persistent accusatory tone. She could hear enthusiastic voices through the closed door, the between-classes bell ringing, and smelled the remnants of Mr. Solomon's lunch in the trash can.

Perseverance realized her world, as she knew it, was drastically about to change, and all the days she ditched school with Daemon to have sex, or to hang with friends, were finally catching up with her.

"Perseverance...are you listening to me?"

"Yes, Mr. Solomon, I'm here," the chair she sat

in squeaked loudly when she shifted her legs.

Mr. Solomon suddenly looked somewhat tired and jaded. This was a typical conversation he had had with many students over the years who did not value his input. He could tell Perseverance had the same laissez-faire attitude as many students who disregarded his guidance. So many of them eventually dropped out of school. Perseverance started this year as a rising senior honor student, so he still hoped his meeting with her would make a difference.

"Okay, Perseverance. Let's get to the point. You have failed so many classes this year you may not graduate from high school. What do you plan to do if you don't graduate?"

Perseverance blurted out, "I plan to go to college."

Mr. Solomon snorted, "You'll never get into any college with these grades. If you don't care about your grades here in high school, why should they bother letting you enroll so you can fail there, too, and prevent a more serious student from getting your seat?"

Perseverance teared up. "Isn't your job supposed to be to help me?"

Mr. Solomon straightened his tie and leaned towards Perseverance.

"I am helping. You are not seeing it through all the negative thoughts in your head. I am presenting reality to you, Perseverance. You have to help yourself first. We can develop a graduation plan, but you must put in the effort. When you first started high school, and we met…you were so much more motivated. What happened to you? Is it that guy I see you with when you are supposed to be in class?"

There was an uncomfortable silence in the room as Perseverance's mind raced to find the words to respond. If Mr. Solomon had seen her outside the school grounds during school hours with Daemon, others would have also seen her. The news would eventually get back to her mom. Should she even open her mouth and explain about Daemon? She couldn't get the words out.

"I have been having a hard time with my dad gone. There is a boy…" she trailed off, not sure what else to say or if anything she did say would make any difference.

Mr. Solomon looked down at the paperwork on his desk and then at Perseverance. "Here is what I'm going to suggest. Go to night school and pick up the extra credits so you can graduate on time. I will hook you up with a specialty counselor for one of the local colleges to get you back on track so you can at least apply to the local community college. They have remedial classes for students that need to get over the hump for some subjects." He paused and looked at her sternly. "Once you show me you are serious."

Perseverance felt the first hope since her father left that house that fateful day. There was a path, a goal, and something over which she had control. She looked at Mr. Solomon and smiled, "Yes, yes, yes – I am serious. I can't *not* graduate this spring. Watch and see just how serious I am."

Mr. Solomon reluctantly smiled back at Perseverance. He couldn't tell if she was responding with a lie or if she was serious about the conversation.

"I know you can do this. Now hurry back to class. I will send the paperwork to your homeroom teacher. You can pick it up tomorrow and get registered by the end of the week. Understand – time is running out. To catch up with your classes, you need to start now, not weeks from now."

Perseverance left Mr. Solomon's office with a new perspective. She was full of hope and inspiration. Even the hallway seemed a little brighter when she returned to class. Just as quickly as her newfound hope had blossomed, she could feel her emotions and the hesitation. The temptation to walk back down the path of self-destruction would never stop. She needed to fight the urge to let go.

She ran into Angie and other close friends, leaving the school campus early to get ready for the basketball game.

"Perseverance! Are you coming over later? We are going to head to my house to carpool from there. Want to meet us?"

"No, Angie. I'll catch up with you all later." Perseverance was eager to get home, finish the day's homework, and look up the local community college to register for evening classes. She was determined to stay focused.

She felt her phone vibrate. It was a text from Daemon demanding she call him. Still frustrated about the night before, she silenced her phone before heading to the next class. She found her seat and pulled out a notebook to take notes.

Her mental attitude to 'do better' started now. Encouraged by Mr. Solomon's guidance, she wrote her favorite scripture, Philippians 4:13, on the outside of her notebook, "I can do all things, through Christ, who strengthens me."

Before her dad moved out, she had enjoyed attending her church's youth group and learning about inspirational scriptures. This scripture stood out; she was ready to see if it was true for herself. After writing down the inspiration, she lifted her head toward the blackboard and the teacher with an open mind, willing and ready to learn the day's lesson.

Perseverance's teacher, Mr. Heppel, was pleasantly surprised to see her engaged in class. Mr. Heppel was a young and energetic history teacher who was passionate about his job and loved finding opportunities for his students to present lessons with their style and flavor.

"Okay, class, I am pairing you with partners for upcoming presentations. I posted the list by the door. Take time to find out who your partner is, introduce yourselves, and pick a topic."

'This is going to be interesting. I haven't been around to do a presentation all semester. I don't know what the teacher is expecting,' Perseverance thought. She watched her classmates excitedly pair up with one another. Since she missed class most of the semester, she didn't know anyone and wondered who her partner was on the list.

Perseverance felt a classmate, Michael, tap her shoulder. "Hey, Perseverance! It's good to see you in class. We are partners on the roster. I wanted to know if you plan to do the assignment. No offense; I just don't want my grade to suffer if you are going to be skipping class." He smiled at Perseverance, and she noticed a dimple in his cheek. "I'll be filling out college applications soon. Since I am not good at math, I need to keep my average up in other subjects."

Embarrassed, Perseverance replied, "Yes, Michael, no worries. I plan on sticking around. No offense taken. I know my class attendance has been a little spotty – but that won't happen again."

Michael smiled with relief. "So, I may have a topic in which you'd be interested. Maybe we can swing by the library after school to do the research. The sooner we start, the better."

Perseverance thought about the basketball game after school and Daemon's constant phone calls, messages, and texts. She thought about what Michael had just said – he was about to apply for college. No one else she hung out with ever talked about that possibility. She had several friends who had missed as much school as she did and barely passed their classes, much less had aspirations for higher education.

Daemon was a high school dropout who only showed up at the high-school campus when he had persuaded Perseverance to leave class to be with him. Now she was faced with Daemon's reality. She was on her way to becoming a high school dropout, too.

"Yes, Michael, I can drive us. Just meet me in the parking lot after school. I have a red Mustang, and it's parked in the front row. Here's my number just in case you can't find me." Perseverance wrote her number on a piece of paper and handed it to him right before the lunch bell rang.

Michael smiled again, revealing deeper dimples in his cheeks, and for the first time, Perseverance took a second look at him. She thought his smile was cute, and as he walked away from her, she noticed how nicely his light blue shirt clung to his athletic-built shoulders. He was tall, confident, and focused. She liked that he looked her in the eyes when they spoke and did not change the subject to see if he could sneak in a kiss. He was a breath of fresh air.

Feeling accomplished after spending the whole day on the high-school campus, Perseverance checked her phone as she headed to her car to meet up with Michael. Her mood instantly turned sour after she saw fifteen missed calls from Daemon. The last few days were the first time she did not respond immediately to his calls since they'd been together.

Still upset, she dismissed the missed call notifications and saw she had a text from Michael. He told her he would be a little late meeting her at the car because he needed to stay after class to talk to his teacher.

She smiled and thought, 'What a nerd,' put the phone back in her purse, and continued walking to her car. She felt proud of herself for sticking through the entire day as she walked across the parking lot. A few students from her history class waved at her as she walked by. She overheard them discussing their project, and she was glad to know about what they were talking.

"This feels good! I feel like a real student again!" She thought to herself before she reached into her purse to get her car keys out.

"So, you ignoring my calls now, huh?"

Perseverance's heart skipped a beat when she recognized Daemon's voice behind her.

"You better have a good reason for not answering my calls," he leaned over her, as she felt her confidence begin to wane.

She looked around; thankfully, most students had sped away from the parking lot as soon as the last bell rang. As she was about to respond, Michael walked up to the car's passenger side. Daemon shoved Perseverance to the side and approached Michael.

"Who is he? Is he why you aren't answering my calls?"

Michael looked towards Perseverance and asked, "Is this a bad time? What's this guy's problem?"

Daemon shoved Michael in the center of his chest and said, "You're the problem! Why are you about to get into my girls' car?"

Michael retreated backward with his hands up in the air, looking at Daemon, then on the ground to find the phone Daemon had knocked out of his hands.

"Hey, man, I don't want any problems with you. I'm just Perseverance's partner for a history project. We were on our way to the library."

Daemon turned back towards Perseverance.

"So we are kicking it with other dudes from class now, huh? Okay, well, we are all going to the library today, then."

Michael stared in puzzlement at Perseverance while Daemon helped himself into the front passenger's seat.

Michael picked up his phone off the ground. "How about we work on our project another time, Perseverance? I have a few ideas I can check out, and I'll let you know what I come up with tomorrow in class."

Perseverance shrugged her shoulders and said, "Okay, I understand. I'm so sorry..."

At that moment, she realized she was in a dead-end...and a dangerous relationship...she couldn't stand to be in it any longer.

She looked at Daemon, anger building up, "Get out of my car – now! I am done with you ordering my friends and me around!" She could feel her eyes flaring, cheeks burning, and a hot flash coursing through her body.

Daemon stared defiantly at her, then slammed his fist on the dashboard before he got out of the car. His eyes were narrowed, and his fists were bawled tight. Perseverance realized things were about to get nasty. She braced for what was to come. Daemon walked over to the driver's side and forcefully opened the door. He reached into the car, grabbed Perseverance's arm, and began to pull her out of the car.

"Is everything okay over there?" A campus officer walked over to the car with a radio in his hand. "Miss, are you in trouble? Is this guy bothering you?"

Before Perseverance could respond, Daemon responded in a smarmy, saccharine voice, "No man, nothing is going on here. I'm just on my way out of here."

The officer watched Daemon stroll over to his Camaro, then drive away with his music blasting far louder than necessary. She watched his car retreating and realized he was knocking his knuckles against the outside of his car door…a habit he had when he was furious and looking for something to hit.

Perseverance got in her car feeling nauseous. She took a sip of water from a water bottle that had been sitting in her cup holder and spit out of the window once she realized the liquid was hot from sitting in the sun all day. She felt awful and sat in the parking lot with the air conditioning blowing on her until she could feel well enough to drive home.

When she pulled into the driveway at home, she realized her mother's car was parked outside, which was unusually early. She put her head down on her steering wheel, breathed a tremendous sigh, and thought. "This day is taking a turn for the worst. I don't feel like dealing with any more drama."

Perseverance turned the engine back on in her car, reversed out of the driveway, and went to her favorite place – the marina. She parked her car by the water and turned on some calming music. She checked her phone to see if she had any missed calls, and surprisingly, she saw none. It was a refreshing change.

Inspired, she pulled out a spiral notebook and searched the Internet on her phone, looking for positive affirmations and encouraging scriptures. She wrote them in her notebook, and after each one, she felt a shift in her mental attitude.

Word by word, she felt a little more hope and joy. As she wrote, the sorrow – and the fear – went away. By sunset, she had a new perspective and pages of inspiration written in her notebook. She decided it was time to drive home and was better prepared to face whatever was going to come her way when she opened the door.

She knew her mother was furious after discussing the missing report cards with the school counselor, Mr. Solomon. Perseverance slowly pulled up to the driveway, turned off the engine to her car, and then muttered to herself, "Let's get this over with…"

After getting the long and well-deserved lecture from her mother and explaining her new goals and attitude to her mother, Perseverance headed towards her room, drained and eager to get into her bed.

Perseverance was jarred awake by the loud alarm clock. She had been so exhausted the night before she had fallen asleep without changing into her pajamas. As she sat up to check the time, her fruit-flavored lip balm fell out of her jeans pocket and onto her bed. Suddenly she felt a sour acid coming up through her throat and nearly pushed her mother over as she ran to the bathroom.

"Perseverance! Is everything alright in there?"

Perseverance was crying and gagging as she threw up in the toilet. Kneeling in front of the porcelain throne and feeling exhausted, her stomach finally gave her a break. Her mother loudly banged on the door. "Perseverance, open this door right now!"

Perseverance crawled to the door and unlocked the doorknob.

"Is there something I need to know? Are you pregnant?"

Perseverance's eyes shot wide open. "Umm. No, why would you say that? I just don't feel good. I think I ate something bad at lunch yesterday."

Her mother looked at her and said, "You're coming with me...now!"

Perseverance thought about Michael and the doubt he already had about her being reliable when it came to the group project. She felt terrible and braced herself on the toilet to lift herself.

"Mom, I need to go to class. I'll be okay."

Her mother yelled, "You missed so many days already; one more day won't hurt you! Get dressed. It won't take me a minute to get an appointment."

"Welcome to the community health center!" The bubbly receptionist greeted Perseverance and her mother, and her smile quickly melted after receiving an icy glare as a response from the unhappy pair.

While her mother completed the patient registration form, Perseverance studied the posters covering the center's wall. Posters provided information about everything from birth control to resources for unplanned pregnancies. Perseverance then looked up to see a pregnant young lady with a belly so large you could see the impression of her navel through her shirt.

"Goodness, she looks exhausted."

Perseverance was feeling nauseous again. A frail, elderly nurse entered the waiting room with a clipboard in her hand and softly called, "Perseverance?"

Perseverance's mother stood up and said, "Over here."

She looked at her daughter and said, "Go Perseverance. I'm not going in with you. You have to make some decisions for yourself."

Perseverance gathered her things and followed the nurse to an examination room.

"Hi, there! My name is Judy. I'll be your nurse today. I hear you need a pregnancy test. When was the last time you had a period?"

Perseverance's memory went blank. She could not believe she was in this position and was asked this question.

"Miss Perseverance, are you okay? If you can't remember, that's okay; just give me an estimate. Has it been more than a month?"

Perseverance realized it could have been almost two months since her last period but didn't think of anything because she was so busy hanging with friends and Daemon. "Yes, it's been more than a month."

The nurse wrote on her notepad, asking, "Have you had unprotected sex?"

Perseverance could not believe the invasive questions but responded hesitantly, "yes."

The nurse nodded, "Okay, that could very well be why you missed your period. I will give you an exam since you clearly haven't had one and answer any questions you may have for me. There's no dumb question, honey; I've heard them all. You will also have some blood work completed so we can check you for other sexually transmitted diseases. I'll step out so you can get undressed from the waist down for your exam. Please put this cover over your lap once you undress."

The nurse quickly left the room, and Perseverance could not believe she was alone in the cold, dimly lit exam room, and possibly pregnant.

"I should be in school right now. How did I allow myself to get into this mess?"

Before undressing for the exam, she checked her phone. Michael had sent her a text asking if she would make it to class today. There were no missed calls from Daemon. That made her sad, especially since she could be pregnant with his child.

After her physical exam, the nurse handed Perseverance a sterile cup and instructed, "Go to the bathroom up the hall and leave a urine sample. Be sure to write your name on it with this pen and leave it on the counter, then stop by the lab for your blood work. I will contact you with the results as soon as I get them. Take care of yourself in the meanwhile. You may need to start taking prenatal vitamins."

The nurse left the room, and Perseverance dressed. She gathered her belongings and headed down the hall to leave a urine sample for her pregnancy test. She saw a clock on the hallway wall and realized she might have enough time to make it to history class. She was determined to follow through on her word to her project partner and was now even more motivated to graduate from high school.

While at the library with Michael, Perseverance heard her phone buzz. Her stomach felt sick when she saw the call from the community health center. She excused herself, walked to a quiet corner, and answered the call.

"Hello, Perseverance; this is Nurse Judy. How are you doing today?"

Perseverance was not up to any small talk, and she wanted Judy to hurry and give her the results. She quickly replied, "I'm fine."

After a brief pause, Judy continued, saying, "Well, I have your lab results, and congratulations, you're pregnant! It looks like you're further than you thought. You're close to three months along."

There was dead silence on the phone.

"Perseverance, are you there? Hello?"

Perseverance was shocked and could not speak, eventually mumbling, "Um, yeah. Thanks."

Nurse Judy realized Perseverance was not excited about the news and did her best to encourage her.

"Look, pregnancy is not always exciting for people; it can be pretty scary for most. I get it. Just know there are plenty of resources out there to help you along. You don't have to do this alone. You signed the consent form for us to refer you to a counselor. I'm going to connect you with a great friend and resource so you can get some additional support. Meanwhile, I will set up your next appointment. You do want to start taking prenatal pills right away. Oh, by the way, the rest of your lab work came out just fine. You are perfectly healthy – what a blessing, especially since you weren't using any protection. I have a few patients who were not as lucky as you are. Take care of yourself and that baby. I'll talk to you soon – have a good day!"

Perseverance disconnected the call – she could not believe the conversation she just had. She felt she needed to be with Daemon for the first time in a while and regretted breaking up with him. She immediately missed him and decided to share the good news.

Perseverance dialed Daemon's number with tears in her eyes. After a few rings, she heard Daemon's favorite song playing in the background. A woman answered the phone, "Hello?"

Perseverance glanced at her phone to ensure she called the correct number and replied, "Is Daemon there?"

She heard Daemon yell, "Aye, why are you on my phone? Give it to me!"

The woman yelled, "Why is there some chick calling your phone? You better tell her to stop calling you!"

Perseverance imagined Daemon checking his caller ID list to see who was calling and could tell he was irritated. "What you want, Perseverance? Why are you calling me?"

Perseverance blurted out, "I'm pregnant, Daemon. I thought you'd like to know."

Daemon laughed and replied, "How I know its mines? It could be that buddy of yours from history class – what's his name again? Anyway, that ain't my problem. We not together anymore, remember?"

Before Perseverance could say anything else, the woman in the background yelled, "Why are you still on the phone? Get rid of her. Hang the phone up! She dumped you anyways!" The phone abruptly disconnected.

She stared at the phone screen, realizing her hopes of going to college were disappearing into a black hole. Now she had to go home and tell her mom the news.

Perseverance slept in the next day after studying all night. Upon waking, she looked at her phone to check the time and realized there was a voicemail. After listening, she called the number back right away. It only took one ring for the phone call to be answered, as though her call was expected.

"Virtuous Community Center, this is Ms. Wisdom speaking."

Perseverance responded by saying, "Hi, Ms. Wisdom, this is Perseverance. I'm returning your call."

Ms. Wisdom's voice lit up like a good friend was calling her, "Oh yes, I'm so glad you called! Nurse Judy referred me to you. She said you gave her consent to be referred to counseling, and they often send patients to me. I hear you are expecting a little blessing! Have you thought of any names?"

Perseverance blinked and reluctantly responded, "I am sort of in a daze right now, so no, I haven't had time to think about names. I haven't even had time to realize I am pregnant right now. It was pretty tough and depressing when I had to tell my mom last night."

Ms. Wisdom paused for a moment, then said, "Listen, dear, I'm not sure what your exact situation is, but I want you to know you don't have to do this alone. My organization has a support group for young pregnant ladies in high school. I'd like to invite you to our meeting tonight. Do you think you could make it?"

Perseverance realized she hadn't told her friends she was pregnant. They wouldn't be able to relate, so she figured it was pointless. She agreed going to Ms. Wisdom's support group might be helpful.

"Yeah, I'll come tonight. And by the way, yes, I've thought of one name. I think I'll name her Purpose if it's a girl."

Perseverance jerked as someone opened her office door. She looked down at the mirror on her desk to realize she was no longer the pregnant teen she was just reminiscing about but a mother of two who now teaches the same class that helped her overcome her struggles.

"Excuse me, Ms. Perseverance, do you mind if I empty your trash cans? I'm sorry to interrupt you. I thought you had already left for the day."

Perseverance looked at the clock, "Oh, my goodness! It's almost time for my next group of students to arrive! I have to get the materials ready for them. I was in deep thought and lost track of time."

Perseverance looked up at the man speaking to her and said, "Wait a minute, aren't you Harmony's grandfather? You're working here now?"

The man chuckled and said, "Yes, I am Harmony's grandfather, and my name is Sam Johnson. I fill in as a janitor until Ms. Wisdom finds a replacement. I'm glad to be of service! Let me get out of your hair so you can prepare for your next class!"

Ms. Perseverance was happy to see another good-hearted person on board. She welcomed Mr. Johnson to the team and rushed to gather supplies.

Chastity

"You're going to be late for school, Chastity! Since when did you spend so much time looking at yourself in the mirror? You're only in the fifth grade!" Perseverance yelled at her youngest daughter as the family rushed around their tiny home before heading to their destinations.

Chastity grumbled as she stomped down the hall toward the kitchen and was greeted with the hustle and bustle of the family's morning routine. The smell of brewing coffee beans was so strong the smell alone woke up anyone who got a whiff. Chastity's sister, Purpose, and their dad were sitting at the table, chuckling about the pre-teen power struggle between Chastity and her mother. Their grits and peppered eggs were steaming on their breakfast plates.

"Mom, why do I have to wear these ponytails in my hair? I am almost 13 years old! These ponytails make me look like a little kid. Can I get my hair flat-ironed? Oh, I know," she excitedly chattered, "Some of those long braids, with colors, like some of my friends? Can you please get me some pants that aren't so short – I look like I am wearing high-water pants...but in a way that isn't trendy at all. I want pants that cover my ankles."

Perseverance looked at Chastity, "Girl, you *are* a little kid! Enjoy being a kid while you can, and the answer is no! The ponytails are staying put! Those pants are in style if you wear them with some confidence! You are a trendsetter, not others around you!"

Chastity stuck her bottom lip out and pouted all the way to the kitchen table.

Perseverance grabbed her lunch out of the refrigerator and looked over at her husband, Michael, "Babe, I have to get to the community center a little early today. Do you mind taking the girls to school this morning?"

Michael looked at her slowly, up and down, enjoying the view of his beautiful wife, "Babe, you just like wine; you get finer with time." He grinned mischievously at his clever line. "Of course, I'll take the girls to school. Don't worry that pretty little face of yours."

Perseverance grinned her appreciation and planted a huge kiss on Michael's forehead.

It had been fifteen years since Michael met Perseverance in their high school history class. She has not changed much in her physical appearance. After having two kids, she had a few stretch marks on her stomach and filled out her jeans with curvier hips. If anything, Michael deeply appreciated her 'mature' appearance as he witnessed her change over the years. On the other hand, Michael's athletic build had rounded out a bit from the nutritious meals Perseverance insisted on cooking daily. His broad shoulders and height camouflaged his round belly when he was dressed. His shirts fell nicely along his torso, and Perseverance liked that he had a little more weight to him. Besides, a bit of pudginess on his cheeks further defined the deep dimples she adored.

"You know, Michael, I always thought you were a nerd in high school, but you turned out to be much cooler than I thought!"

Everyone in the kitchen erupted into laughter. Chastity tried to hold on to her angry face as long as possible while they ignored her, but she couldn't hold it any longer. She surrendered to the laughter that bubbled up, which released the tension in the atmosphere between her and her mother.

Michael replied, "Girls, you should've seen how cool I was years ago."

Turning to Perseverance, he added, "Let's not talk about that night I danced circles around you... remember our first night out in college together. All the ladies had their eyes on me that night!"

Perseverance playfully threw the kitchen towel at Michael, "Oh, please, let's talk more about these ladies. I was in class with a few of them, remember?"

Michael chuckled, pushing his chest out boastfully, "Yeah, I was the man..."

Perseverance laughed and rolled her eyes, "Whatever!"

Purpose finally caught her breath from laughing and said, "Dad, you're still a big nerd!"

Michael snorted through a mouthful of coffee and reached for the dish towel to catch the drips from his chin.

Perseverance gave Purpose a high five. "Okay, I love you all. Be nice! Let's all have a good day today!" She giggled on her way out the door, grateful for the family with which she'd been blessed.

As Perseverance left, Michael and the girls scooted their chairs away from the table and gathered their belongings. Michael cleared his throat and swallowed his last spoonful of grits, "Come on, girls, let's head to the car. You don't want to be late for school."

Michael parallel parked his Chrysler in front of Chastity's school, "Okay, sweetheart, do well in school today. Your mother is teaching a teen-parenting class tonight, so you need to be ready to go when the bell rings. Love you!"

Michael waved goodbye to his daughter and watched her walk into her school. He thought, 'She sure looks like her mother,' as he pulled the car away from the curb."

As Chastity walked towards the front of the school and up the stairs, she heard her best friend, Samantha, call her name.

"Chastity! Hey, wait for me!"

She turned to see Samantha trotting up the stairs, wearing skinny jeans and a slim-fit jacket, looking both stylish and radiant. Samantha's hair was flat-ironed, and the paint on her nails matched the highlights in her hair.

Chastity looked her friend up and down, sighing with admiration and jealousy. Samantha's mom owned the Glamourous Beauties hair shop and nail spa. Everyone in town raved about the shop and how good they looked after Samantha's mom worked on them.

"I see your mother made you wear those ponytails to school – again!" Samantha giggled as she made it up the last set of stairs.

Chastity frowned, unsure if she or her situation was being teased. "Yeah, apparently, I'm still considered a little kid."

"Come on, Chastity, let's go to the bathroom. I brought some stuff to do your hair, just in case. Today is not the day to look like a little kid."

Before Chastity could ask her what was so special about today, Samantha grabbed her arm and led her to the girls' bathroom. Samantha unzipped her jacket, showing off her form-fitting shirt, which revealed her blooming body. She was much more developed than Chastity, who was a bit heavier. Chastity was always told that she got her 'big bones' from her dad's side of the family.

Samantha looked at Chastity and said, "Okay, let's hurry and get these ponytails out of your head before class starts. Come on, help me."

Chastity stared at her hair in the mirror, trying to memorize how her mother did it so she could place the ponytails back where they belonged before leaving school. Samantha manipulated and brushed Chastity's thick, soft hair into a more mature-looking messy bun. She then grabbed some towels from the bathroom dispenser and balled them up to soften the crunchy paper.

"Stick this in your bra, girl. Put this lip gloss on your lips."

Chastity pulled her shirt neckline down far enough to stuff the paper into her 'trainer bra,' trying to readjust the crunchy towels so they wouldn't scratch and make crackly noises as she moved. In minutes, Chastity watched herself transform into a busty-looking young woman.

"Why are we getting all dressed up right now?"

Samantha looked around nervously and checked under the stall doors to ensure no one else was in the bathroom, "We were invited to play a game with the sixth graders during lunch today. Well...I was invited, but you're my best friend, and I can't leave you out! We do everything together, ever since the second grade, remember?"

Concerned, Chastity turned to look Samantha sternly in the eyes, and said, "What game are you talking about, Samantha? One of those games behind the school in the bushes where Principal Rubie said no one is allowed?

Samantha shared a devious grin, "Exactly! Relax, Chastity...I have a personal invitation. Don't you want to hang with Jessie and her crew? She is so popular, and it would be so cool to hang out with her."

Chastity thought about what her mother often said before she went to school. "You are a trendsetter, not others around you." For some reason, those words were not as annoying as they had seemed earlier.

Chastity looked at herself in the mirror, patted her hair, and nervously picked at the curves of her newly enlarged bust.

"Jessie is one of the most popular girls in the school, but I heard she did things to get that title. Things I don't feel comfortable doing."

Samantha's face sagged, clearly upset with Chastity's response, and she shoved the hair supplies into her backpack.

"I'm going to hang with the sixth graders today. I am ready to grow up and show it. I don't care if you come or not with your attitude." Samantha huffed out of the bathroom and headed to class.

Chastity felt she was losing her best friend. It didn't feel right. She fluffed up the paper towel tissues in her bra again, grabbed her backpack, and headed to class. When she walked into the classroom, she caught some boys responding with double glances – checking out her new look.

Ryan, her secret crush, approached her, "Hey, Chastity, are you going to play kickball with us today at lunch? You can be on my team if you'd like."

Chastity looked towards Samantha's seat, saw her passing notes back and forth with Jessie, and replied, "Um, today may not be good. Is tomorrow okay?"

Ryan looked away in embarrassment, obviously feeling rejected, "Sure, Chastity, that's cool."

She liked the extra attention she was getting. Maybe hanging with the popular kids wouldn't be so bad after all. She whispered to Samantha just before the teacher clacked a ruler on her desk for the class's attention, "Okay, I'll go with you to play the game at lunch. We're besties, and I can't leave you hanging."

Chastity smiled and nodded at Samantha before sitting at her desk.

She overheard Jessie whisper, "Oh my gosh, Sammie, is she wearing that today? Who wears pants like that? Does she shop at a thrift store or something?"

The small cluster of girls covered their mouths as they giggled. Chastity mustered up an awkward smile to hide her discomfort. She glanced back at Samantha. Chastity was saddened, and a little jealous, to see how much fun Samantha and Jessie seemed to have talking to each other.

Since Mrs. Yee changed the seating chart around, it seemed like those two were growing closer daily. Chastity looked up at the clock in anticipation of the lunch break. Today she would skip the line for a hot meal in the cafeteria and stay outside with the other students who had brought their packed lunch. She couldn't wait to share a fresh experience with her bestie and play the game about which Samantha was so excited.

"Rinnng!" The lunch bell clanged, and Chastity rushed toward Samantha and the group of girls around her. She glanced at Ryan to catch him looking at her from across the room. She shyly waved to him as she followed the group of girls. She was more motivated to tag along with the popular girls and tried to sway her hips just like they did, regardless of how awkward she looked while walking.

As the group of girls walked across the schoolyard, Samantha nudged Chastity's arm and discreetly whispered, "Your tissue is lopsided."

Chastity stood behind Samantha and quickly slipped her hand up her shirt to put her tissue back in place. When the coast was clear, the girls slid through a hole in the side fence, leading to a secluded area surrounded by bushes. About seven girls and eight boys sat in a circle in the hot sun, squirming with excitement.

Jessie loudly said, "Okay, everyone, this is Chastity and Samantha. They came to play our game with us today." Jessie was a fashionable and full-figured young lady. Her trendy outfit consisted of leggings and a t-shirt cropped enough to reveal her belly ring. Those not admiring Jessie's belly ring stared quietly at Chastity and Samantha for a brief moment while the girls sat down.

Jessie put her hands on her hips, "Alright, everybody, let's get started... we don't have much time before the bell rings."

"You know the deal. We are playing Hide and Go Get it, and whatever 'get it' means to you and who you find is your business. Remember to stay in this area, so the yard teacher doesn't catch us and give us detention. The game starts *now!*"

Samantha eagerly smiled at Chastity and dashed off with a brief wave. Chastity lingered behind, unsure of what to do. What was the purpose of this game?

'I'd rather be playing dodgeball with Ryan,' she thought.

"Run, Chastity! Pimple Face is coming for you!" Jessie yelled, giggled, and ran in the opposite direction.

Chastity was confused and thought to herself, 'Pimple face? Who is that? Oh – wait, Edgar, the one who started puberty and has pimples and craters oozing all over the place. Oh, no!'

"Tag! I got you, Chastity! Now give me my kiss!" Edgar smiled, and as his mouth curled upwards, a whitehead oozed from one of his pimples.

Chastity didn't know what to do and panicked, shaking her head, thinking desperately, 'No, this cannot be my first kiss – not this way. Not him!'

Edgar ignored the disgust on her face. He leaned in, and Chastity looked closely at what appeared to be a third eye on his nose. A ripe pimple seemed to be yelling, "Pop me and put me out of my misery, please!"

Chastity panicked and ran away, screaming towards the playground. Her yelling drew the attention of the yard teachers, who quickly blew their whistles.

"Chastity, where are you coming from? Why are you on that side of the school when it's off-limits?"

The commotion was so loud it interrupted the kickball game in the schoolyard. Embarrassed, Chastity put her head down, wishing she could disappear. The yard teachers, Ms. Crusher and Mr. Bats, walked to Chastity and started questioning her, which drew even more attention from the other kids on the playground. While the yard teachers interrogated Chastity, some other kids used the opportunity to sneak away from the hiding spot so they wouldn't get caught.

As Chastity's accomplices tried to sneak away, Mr. Bats blew his whistle at them while yelling, "I see you! We will come for you next!"

Mr. Bats was only five feet two inches tall, and about 260 pounds. His ankles rolled over the sides of his tennis shoes, and as he tried to run after the kids coming from the bushes, the other kids on the playground laughed hysterically at his failed attempt at speed. While Ms. Crusher wrote Chastity a detention slip, Mr. Bats waddled back to inspect the area Chastity had run from in the bushes.

"Rinnng" The bell rang, and kids came swarming from everywhere on the playground towards the school building. Chastity's stomach was in knots, and she felt her heart sink. She may have gotten Samantha and all the popular kids in school in trouble. Her actions were going to ruin her chances at popularity forever. Samantha made her way to her classroom and sat down in her seat.

The bell rang again, signaling the end of lunch break, prompting her teacher to order the class to settle down. Jessie's and Samantha's seats were empty. Empty seats were not good. The kids in the class were unusually rowdy and whispering back and forth.

Chastity couldn't hear what they were saying behind their hands. As she tried her best to focus on the teacher's lecture and her classmates' whispered conversations, her thoughts were interrupted by her classmate, Katie.

"Did you hear what happened at lunch, Chastity?" Katie tapped impatiently on Chastity's shoulder a few times from behind Chastity's seat in class. "Chastity...did you hear me?"

Chastity ignored Katie and watched as the door to the classroom swung open. The principal came into the classroom, followed by Samantha and Jessie, looking sheepish and a little red-faced. Both girls wore sweats and tee shirts imprinted with the school's mascot, a ram. This was the standard school-issued outfits for students who were caught wearing non-conformance-to-school-policy outfits to school.

Chastity wondered to herself – what happened to Samantha and Jessie? The students in the class continued to whisper and giggle, staring hard at the two girls.

"Everyone settle down now – the show is over. Open your textbooks to chapter three," Mrs. Yee sternly spoke to the class as she peered over the rim of her glasses at the students, visually daring anyone to act up.

Samantha avoided making eye contact with Chastity for the rest of the day. On the other hand, Jessie made a point to stare intensely at Chastity with a threatening gaze. Chastity bit her lip, feeling she might be in trouble later, but she couldn't figure out what Jessie would do. She felt she might not want to be caught by any kids involved in the game after school. Who knows what they would do? Would they gang up on her or challenge her to a fight? She had never gotten into a physical altercation with anyone before.

She waited until everyone was silently reading in class, quietly walked over to Mrs. Yee, and asked if she could have a hall pass and go to the bathroom. The hall pass was an oversized wooden paddle with the words' hall pass' written in big black letters. This let school staff know whoever was holding it had permission to be out of class.

While walking through the hallway, Chastity saw Ryan walking down the opposite side, looking at her differently than he usually did – in barely disguised disgust. Chastity waved at Ryan and said, "Hi." Ryan responded by shaking his head in disappointment, looking away, and kept on walking.

Chastity was caught off guard at his look.

"Ryan! What's wrong? Why are you looking at me like that?"

Ryan, clearly bothered, turned around, talking as he continued to walk backward but away from her, "I heard about the game you and your friends played at lunch...Edgar...of all people, Chastity?"

Chastity was confused and said, "What? Nothing happened between Edgar and me! I didn't even know what that game was about until everyone started running around, and I left!"

Ryan stopped walking away from Chastity and said, "That's not what he's telling people. Samantha was found half-naked in the bushes with Dwayne. What's going on with you two? I thought you were different, Chastity." He shook his head again. "I have to go."

Chastity was at a loss for words...what had just happened? In the space of two hours, her entire life had changed entirely. She wanted the braids her mother put in her head back and rushed to the bathroom. She pulled her hair out of the messy ponytail and ripped the lopsided tissue out of her training bra. Then she remembered Samantha had all of her hair bows in her backpack. Chastity knew she couldn't ask for them back now. Samantha probably won't ever talk to her again!

She reached in her pocket, hoping she would find a few hair bows, and instead found the detention slip the yard teacher gave her. She was scheduled to sit on the bench during lunch for the rest of the week.

"I got myself into a big mess today," Chastity said with a loud sigh. She took a deep breath, opened the bathroom door, and headed back to class.

The last bell rang, and Chastity tried her best to rush out of class before Jessie and Samantha could approach her. The class was loud, and a few kids threw paper balls across the room. Mrs. Yee was yelling last-minute homework reminders over the loud chatter. Chasity tuned out the commotion and shoved her binder into her backpack. She managed to make it out the door and towards the stairs. As she was about to place her foot on a step, her body was violently thrown backward after someone tugged one of her backpack straps so hard she fell. While Chasity was on the ground, someone ripped her backpack from her shoulders.

"Where are you going so fast, 'Big Bertha'?" Jessie was standing right behind her.

Chastity answered quickly, "Look. I didn't mean to get everyone in trouble. I was trying to get away from Edgar."

Jessie and her clique of girls laughed and said, "Well, from what we heard, you didn't try that hard to get away."

Everyone in the hallway laughed. Chastity caught Ryan shaking his head out of the corner of her eye as he continued down the stairs toward the school exit. Her hopes for developing any type of relationship with him sunk.

Chastity was getting upset and said, "Give me my backpack now, Jessie!"

Samantha jerked Chastity's backpack out of Jessie's hands, "Leave her alone, you guys. I know her. She wouldn't have gotten us into trouble on purpose. I don't want to get into any more trouble. Leave her alone!"

Chastity looked at Samantha with a face full of gratitude and reached her hand out for her backpack. Chastity whispered to Samantha, "Thank you. I'm so sorry."

Looking at the time on her wristwatch, Chastity headed outside to meet her mother, waiting in the parking lot.

When Chastity approached the car, Perseverance rolled down the driver's window to fuss at her.

"What happened to your hair, Chastity? So, you got rid of the ponytails anyway, I see. I got a call from your principal today. What happened at lunch? Are you still hanging out with that girl? What's her name again? Samantha? I told you she was trying to grow up way too fast! Get in the car now!"

Chastity quietly said, "I'm sorry, mom," and remained quiet for the rest of the ride to the Virtuous Community Center.

The silence broke once they arrived at the center, and Perseverance parked the car. "While I am teaching a class tonight, you two are to sit quietly in the break room and work on your homework. We will talk when we get home, Chastity."

As they got out of the car, Mr. Johnson, who was raking the leaves, greeted them. Purpose asked her mom, "Isn't that Harmony's grandpa? He works here now?"

Perseverance replied, "Yes, dear, he does."

Mr. Johnson grinned and said, "Good afternoon, ladies! I see you have a new hairstyle, Chastity! No more ponytails?"

Chastity nervously smiled.

Perseverance replied, "No sir, not for long. The ponytails will be coming back!"

Mr. Johnson laughed and raked the leaves into a large garbage bag.

Purpose and Chastity sat quietly in the break room until they were certain their mother was in her classroom.

Purpose looked at Chastity and asked, "What were you thinking today? Why all the drama?"

Chastity sharply said, "I don't feel like talking about it, Purpose, leave me alone."

Purpose shrugged her shoulders and pulled her math book out of her backpack, "I'll be right back. I'm heading to the kitchen to see if I can find us something to eat."

As Purpose opened the door, Honesty nearly ran into her.

"Oops! Sorry, Purpose!"

Honesty laughed while carrying two heavy suitcases through the door and into the break room. She set the suitcases against the wall and looked up,

"Hey, Chastity? Cute hair!"

Chastity replied, "Please don't mention my hair. I am already in enough trouble with my mom!"

Honesty replied, "Oh, I'm sorry. Is everything okay?"

Chastity needed to get things off her chest and told Honesty about the incident at school. It shocked Honesty to hear that Chastity, the daughter of Perseverance, could even end up in that compromising situation.

Once Chastity finished telling the story, Honesty nodded to her face showing she understood perfectly. "Do you know why I ended up staying here in the first place?"

Chastity replied, "No, not really. I just thought that you really, and I mean *really*, enjoyed being here, so you moved in."

Honesty laughed. "No, that's not it. I mean, I really do like this place, but…I had no choice. My mom kicked me out."

Chastity's mouth dropped, thinking, 'How could a mother kick her own daughter out of the house?'

Honesty shared her story of how she met an older guy online, lied about her age, and how she met up with him. She explained, "That was one of the worst days of my life and one of the biggest mistakes I've ever made. I was determined to grow up and be what I thought was a mature woman; I didn't see I was childish, naïve, and stupid. It's best to stay true to who you are and recognize your worth. Try not to grow up too fast."

"It's funny we are talking about this now. My mother and I worked things out, and she's on her way to pick me up. Things aren't perfect, but our relationship with one another is going in the right direction. I finally feel like she sees me. She's letting me move back in with her. I've grown and gotten a heck of a lot smarter about the world since being here with Ms. Wisdom. I realize there are people out there who will try to take advantage of young girls like us who don't know any better, even though they think they do. I know better now."

Chastity realized she wasn't the only person who had issues with their mother.

Honesty then pulled her sleeve up to show Chastity an engraved bracelet on her wrist. It was a simple design with the words 'I am a Jewel.'

"You see, Chastity, this is one of the first things Ms. Wisdom said to me. She called me a jewel. I finally see that for myself when I look in the mirror. It took me a while, but I *get it* now."

She looked at Chastity and said, "Before I go, I want to give you something."

Honesty grabbed a small bag from her suitcase and brought them to the table where Chastity was sitting. "I got this the other day from the mall. I think they would be perfect for you." Honesty handed Chastity a pair of earrings shaped like lotus flowers.

"The day I went to the mall to buy these earrings, my science teacher talked about the lotus flower and what makes it special. She said these flowers bloom in muddy waters, unstained by the filth surrounding the plant, and maintains its purity - despite where it is growing. Every night, it closes its petals and sinks into the muddy water, only to rise and open its beautiful pedals the next day."

Honesty looked into Chastity's eyes, "You remind me of a lotus flower. Although you may have gotten into muddy waters today, you still rose beautifully and purely. Yes, this Edgar guy may have made your choice easy this time because you were not attracted to him, but what if it is not as easy for you the next time? I hope you will continue to choose to rise like the lotus flower whenever you find yourself in a muddy situation, especially when it comes to making choices with your body."

Chastity held her gift in the palm of her hand, touched by the beauty of the gift. "Thank you, Honesty. Thank you, so much!"

Honesty's sister, Charity, stepped into the break room and said, "There you are! Mom is in Ms. Wisdom's office, ready to go. I can't wait to show you what I've done to my room while you were gone!"

The girls waved goodbye to Chastity.

"Hey, sis! I found us some food. Sorry I took so long. The kitchen was busy serving people from the community, so I had to wait my turn." Purpose strode into the room with a tray of steaming plates of hot spaghetti noodles, meatballs, and a couple of soda cans.

"Thank you," Chastity responded. The two sisters enjoyed their meal together and worked on homework while waiting for their mom.

While finishing their homework, they heard their dad talking on the phone while walking up the hall.

He poked his head through the breakroom door, "Here are my princesses!" He then looked at Chastity. "Come and walk with me, baby girl."

Chastity knew he had heard about what happened at school and was bracing for a lecture as she walked toward her dad. He lovingly put his hands around her shoulder and said, "I just want to spend a little time with you. I know what happened today, and I see you found a way to get rid of those ponytails. Don't tell your mom, but I think your hair looks nice like this!" He smiled, showing off the deep dimples her mother so loved.

Chastity giggled and felt a little relief about the direction the conversation with her dad was going. They found a bench outside, nestled between a few trees, and sat down, enjoying the little bit of sun left for the day. It was a hot spring day, and the shade provided by the trees was delightful. Chastity swung her legs back and forth as she sat on the bench.

"Chastity, I want you to know that you aren't the first or the last young lady to face the challenges you faced today. Has your mother spoken to you about today yet?"

Chastity shook her head and said, "No."

Michael nodded his head and said, "I figured. She probably won't say much, to be honest. I'll let her know I spoke with you, just in case. I want you to know you're not much different from your mother, which may be why it's challenging for her to talk to you about certain things. It's easier for her to deal with kids that aren't her own than to look someone in the face who looks like a younger version of herself. I met her when she was young and witnessed some of her challenges. The best part is, I witnessed her overcome those challenges...just like I know you will."

Michael pulled out his phone and searched for a scripture. "I'm going to make this quick. Here it is, 1 Corinthians 6:19-20; it talks about your body being a temple. Do you understand what that means? As a Christian, your body is a temple and dwelling place for God. You must treat it with love and respect and honor it. Does that make sense? You are royalty, honey, and your body is to be treated as such. Remember that, okay? When Purpose was your age, I had the same talk with her, and she got it. I hope the same for you. If you need to talk, I am always here for you.

Chastity smiled, nodded her head, and hugged her dad. They heard the back door open and saw Perseverance waving.

Michael waved back, "Looks like your mom is done. Let's get home and enjoy the rest of the evening."

The next day, Perseverance woke the girls up earlier than usual. "Come on, girls, time to get up. I'll be driving you to school today."

Chastity yawned, feeling her stomach growl as her nostrils sucked in the delicious aroma of fresh pancakes wafting from the kitchen. She smiled. Her mom played Chastity's favorite Christian band and sang along with some overly energetic Christian praise in the background. Her dad was reading the morning paper at the head of the table, a few pancake crumbs littering his plate next to an empty coffee cup.

After breakfast, Chastity asked, "Mom, can you do my hair today?" She looked forward to sitting on the edge of her mother's bed while her mom braided her ponytails.

Perseverance was surprised, "Of course, I can, sweetie. I was going to let you do your own hair today, but if you insist," she trailed off.

Chastity giggled, "Mom, you were right. I think I will enjoy just being a kid as long as I can."

Perseverance grinned and whispered, "Thank you, Jesus!"

Michael chimed in, "Amen to that, darling! Believe me; you won't regret it!"

After breakfast, everyone made their way to the car. Chastity confidently walked to the car with her awkward fitting pants, ponytails, and lotus flower earrings. Although things were okay at home, she still had to face everyone at school. She was ready to get it over with, regardless of how things turned out.

Perseverance pulled up to the curb at Chasity's school. After Chastity got out of the car, she waited a while before she drove off, curiously watching what Chastity's next steps would be. She watched Chastity walk towards the steps leading to the school's front entrance. Perseverance was surprised to see Samantha sitting on the bottom steps of the school stairs with her head full of ponytails.

Samantha looked up at Chastity and said, "Look at what my mother did to my hair!" as she burst into tears. Samantha's nail polish was also gone, and she wore a stylish, but below-the-knee dress – something more suitable for attending church than school.

Samantha stood up and said, "Look at me, Chastity! My mom took all of my cute clothes away. She said I was trying to grow up too fast and I needed to focus more on school than how I looked. What's wrong with her? I look just like…you! I hate it!"

Shocked, Chastity put her hands on her hips. "Now, wait a minute; you're taking this too far! It's not my fault you got caught in the bushes!"

Samantha wiped her eyes and groaned, "I'm so sorry, Chastity. It's been a rough couple of days. Let's get to class before I get into any more trouble. I confronted Edgar yesterday after school when my big brother came to pick me up. I know he was lying about what happened between you two. My brother scared him into confessing the truth." Samantha smiled. "He tried to play everything off like he was just kidding, which is not cool. So that you know, my brother told Edgar he needed to 'fess up and tell everybody the truth at school' – *or else*. So the real truth will get out."

Chastity was relieved that, deep down, Samantha was still a loyal best friend regardless of what happened. While walking to class, Chastity saw Ryan in the hallway. She quickly looked in a different direction to avoid an awkward conversation until she heard him call her name.

"Chastity! Hey, wait up!"

Samantha kept walking and said, "I can't risk being late for class. I need my other clothes back before my reputation is ruined forever!"

Chastity laughed and waited for Ryan to run up the hallway toward her.

"Hey, Chastity, I wanted to apologize for what I said to you yesterday. I heard Edgar admitted the rumors were not true about you and him. If you're still up to it, there's room on my kickball team if you want to play at lunch."

Chastity pulled her detention slip out of her pocket and said, "I wish I could, but I have a meeting with the bench for lunch. Maybe next week."

Ryan nodded his head and said, "Okay, that sounds good. Let's get to class before the bell rings. Maybe I can sit on the bench with you today?"

They both laughed and rushed down the hall to class.

Purpose

"Mom! There is someone at the door for you!" Chastity yelled down the hall.

Michael was in the kitchen and got up from the table to check who was at the door.

"I'll get it, Chastity; your mom is in the shower."

Chastity was confused when she saw her dad's facial reaction when he glanced through the glass door pane. She peeked over his shoulder to see who it was. There was something familiar about the man's facial features, but she couldn't quite put a finger on it. Purpose looked up from the breakfast table.

Michael sternly told his daughters, "Girls, go to your room."

This seemed serious. Chastity was curious to find out who this person was and looked at her sister with a quizzical look on her face. Both girls moved towards the hallway, looking behind them on the way to their room.

Michael stepped outside the house and closed the door behind him.

Purpose and Chastity veered into the living room and peeked out the window to see their father waving his arms around, obviously agitated in the conversation with the stranger. The girls could barely hear what the commotion was about. Their dad was upset, and this was a side of their father they hardly ever saw.

Perseverance walked into the living room behind the girls. "What are you two doing? What are you looking at?" Once she saw the stranger through the window, she gasped.

"Daemon?" She whispered in surprise and quickly walked out the front door to join Michael on the front sidewalk, leaving the door slightly ajar behind her.

"What are you doing here? How did you find out where I lived?"

The girls hovered at the front door, straining to hear the conversation. Purpose whispered to avoid being overheard by her parents, "Who is Daemon? What's going on?" her sister shrugged, just as confused. They watched the stranger give their mom a piece of paper.

The stranger yelled, "I just want to see my daughter! I'll see you in court!" He stomped his feet and then turned and walked away, getting into a raggedy, older model car and cranking up the stereo as he peeled away from the curb.

Michael and Perseverance shook their heads in disbelief as they watched the angry man turn right at the top of the neighborhood street. They walked back towards the house and into the front door. Purpose and Chastity saw their parents had worried looks on their faces.

Perseverance looked at Purpose and sighed.

"Baby girl, that was your biological dad. My ex-boyfriend from high school."

Purpose said, "What! Why won't you let me see him?"

She ran outside, but Daemon was long gone. She ran back into the house and yelled, "What's wrong with you guys? Why didn't you let him speak to me?"

Perseverance replied, "We were protecting you, Purpose. It's been a long time, and he wasn't the nicest person to be around. As far as I can tell, he is still not nice. I don't know if it's safe for you to be with him. I don't know him anymore."

Frustrated, Purpose whined, "Oh, it's okay for Chastity to know her real dad, but not me! That's not fair!"

Michael retorted, "What was that supposed to mean? I *am* a real dad to you."

Purpose ran to her room crying and closed the door.

The next few days, Purpose had very few words for her parents and went about her daily routine showing very little emotion. Purpose found herself watching Chastity and Michael spending time together, secretly wishing she could get to know her biological dad. She had hoped to have a chance to get a good look at him and see what features they had that were similar.

She kept thinking, "Do I have his eyes or his toes? Mine don't favor mom's, too much." Purpose did her best to process things on her own. She tried journaling in her diary but seemed to burst into tears after a few paragraphs. Her pillow was soggy from her bouts of crying.

After thinking about the situation for a few days, she realized she was getting nowhere with self-pity. She was ready to hear her mother's side of the story. She also wanted to listen to the plan to get to know her biological dad.

Perseverance cautiously approached Purpose the next morning, ready for any negative response. "Are you ready to talk now?"

Purpose responded by nodding her head, knowing the conversation's topic.

Perseverance sat on the giant bean bag in Purpose's room.

"I told you. Your biological dad and I did not have a good relationship. In fact, it was selfish, demanding, and one-sided on his behalf. When I discovered I was pregnant, he was not there for me. He ran away and told me, 'it was my problem now, not his.' I was lost, confused, and at a low point in my life. I knew I did want to keep my baby – you. Michael was a classmate at school; he was there for me during my darkest period. And looking forward to you being born gave me a...purpose...in life. That's how I named you."

Purpose sat up, ignoring the point of the conversation.

"But, mom, my dad came looking for me. That's all that matters!"

Perseverance's face fell, showing her disappointment that Purpose didn't understand her point of view. She sighed with resignation.

"Purpose, I will allow you to see him as long as we are there with you. He left his contact information. We will call and arrange a meeting in a public location."

Purpose beamed with joy and gave her mom an enormous hug. "Oh my gosh, thank you, thank you, thank you, mom!"

Perseverance warmed up, seeing Purpose smiling again. Her biggest worry was Daemon would disappoint his daughter as much as he had disappointed her fifteen years ago. She was worried her daughter's vibrant spirit would be crushed, and the situation would be more challenging than when Daemon rebuked her years ago. On the other hand, Perseverance did not want to circumvent the potential for a positive outcome either.

She silently prayed, 'Lord, please help me,' as she walked back to her room to call Daemon and make arrangements. Daemon's voice, over the phone, brought back a flood of memories and feelings she thought she was numb to after so many years. That night Perseverance tossed and turned in her bed with worry. She struggled with the painful memories caused by Daemon – his violent threats, his verbal abuse, and the emotional pain he forced her through years ago. It haunted her, and she was worried about her daughter being exposed to the same painful emotions.

Perseverance woke up with puffy eyes and a headache. She crawled out of bed and dressed, then walked downstairs to the kitchen. Michael and the girls were already eating breakfast.

"Michael, do you mind taking the girls to the mall today? Ms. Wisdom needs me to fill in at the office for her. She hasn't been feeling well lately."

Michael could tell Perseverance was worried, "Anything serious?"

Perseverance nervously bit the corner of her mouth, "I sure hope not. If it is, she wouldn't tell me, anyway. She doesn't like it when I worry about her. She's been out of the office a lot lately, however. Please, help Purpose find something appropriate to wear for her meeting with Daemon."

Purpose's face lit up as she chewed on a spoonful of cereal. Chastity looked at her sister with a tiny bit of envy.

Perseverance's face scrunched up; her tiny age-related wrinkles more pronounced after mentioning Daemon's name. Perseverance caught Michael looking at her with concern on his face. She kissed Michael, "I'll be fine. Ms. Wisdom will be fine. Purpose will be fine. We will get through this."

Michael admonished the girls as they finished their breakfast, "Come on, ladies, let's get moving. You have some serious damage to do to my bank account!"

The girls giggled.

Purpose was too excited to eat, "I'm done. Let's go!"

They grabbed their jackets, and their busy chatter spilled through the front door on the way to the mall.

While her family was shopping at the mall, Perseverance was busy filing documents in Ms. Wisdom's office. She ran across a red envelope with the words "Final Notice" stamped across the front. Perseverance opened it and found a foreclosure notice for the Virtuous Community Center. Her mouth fell.

"She's behind thirty thousand dollars! Why didn't she say anything to us?" she exclaimed to what she thought was an empty room. The sound of a throat clearing behind her caused her to spin around to see Mr. Johnson at the door.

"Hi, Mr. Johnson; how are you doing? Have you heard from Ms. Wisdom?"

Mr. Johnson didn't look like his usual spunky self. The lines around his eyes were more profound, and his shoulders sagged.

He shook his head, "She's been admitted to the hospital. They are going to have to keep her overnight to monitor her. Since I'm not her spouse or family, they won't disclose anything about her medical condition. And she won't tell me. I'm sorry I don't have more for you."

Perseverance was shocked to hear the news, but at the same time, glad someone else genuinely cared about Ms. Wisdom. She shared the bad news about the foreclosure notice. "This is just between you and me. Don't tell anyone else; it may upset Ms. Wisdom that we even know about it."

Mr. Johnson nodded, "Things make more sense now. I wonder if the stress was just too much for her health." He put forth a feeble smile. "Don't worry. I will check on her daily while you take care of things here. I will keep you posted."

Perseverance took a deep breath, "I know she doesn't have much family in the local area. I appreciate you. I'll check on her when I can and try to see if I can assist with contacting her family--if she wants my help."

Perseverance placed the foreclosure notice back in the envelope and put it in the top drawer of Ms. Wisdom's desk, along with a stack of other bills. She wanted to ensure the bad news was not in sight of other visitors. She spent the remainder of the afternoon organizing the office, which distracted her mind from worrying thoughts. What felt like minutes later, she looked up at the clock and saw it was already 5:00 in the evening. It was time to go home. She gathered her belongings and locked up the office.

Perseverance opened the front door to her home and found her husband patiently sitting in the kitchen, waiting with a warm plate of leftovers on the table. Perseverance's face lit up as she kicked off her heels, hung her coat on a hook by the back door, and slid into the chair next to his. They leaned towards each other for a tender hello kiss.

"Thank you, love; I didn't realize how hungry I was until I smelled this food. Mm-mmm. You know my favorite dish! Collard greens, smoked turkey neck, and black-eyed peas." She sighed. "It's been a long, busy day."

"Relax honey, just eat so that you can get some rest. We have a big day in the morning." Michael rubbed her back for a few seconds, then leaned back in his chair. He looked at Perseverance with concern and asked, "Have you talked to Purpose about the plans to meet up with Daemon yet?"

"Don't remind me about Daemon – I can't believe he showed up the way he did! Why does he decide to show up at all – and now? Where was he when I needed his help?" She paused and said, "To answer your question, yes, I did let Purpose know about the meet-up scheduled for tomorrow." She continued, "I wonder if it has anything to do with him possibly getting tax deductions or just something in his soul has realized he needs to be a real father to his daughter.

Michael put his hand on Perseverance's shoulder, his voice soothing her mood, "Everything will be okay. Just let Purpose figure out who he is for herself. That's the best thing to do. Don't worry; I'm here for you. Daemon doesn't matter. Purposes' real father is sitting right next to you."

Perseverance smiled warmly, wiped a tear from her eye, and picked up her fork. As she put a spoonful of buttery black-eyed peas in her mouth, she realized the conversation about Daemon caused her to lose her appetite.

She put her napkin over her plate and said, "I'm sorry, babe, but I just don't have an appetite like I thought I did. Daemon has got me too upset to eat. I'm going to try to get some rest now. Please put my plate in the fridge when you get a moment." She pushed her chair away from the table and headed to their bedroom.

Perseverance woke up to a gentle nudge from Michael. "Good Morning, honey; you have a phone call. It's Ms. Wisdom. Get dressed so that we aren't late for our meeting."

Perseverance quickly sat up in bed, picked up the phone, "Hello…Ms. Wisdom. I heard the hospital kept you overnight. We were so worried about you! Are you doing okay?"

Ms. Wisdom assured Perseverance that she would leave the hospital 'soon,' but would have to stay home for bed rest until the doctor allowed her back to work. She thanked Perseverance for filling in for her at the community center and noted some of her close family members could come into town to help.

Before they disconnected the call, Ms. Wisdom still managed to lift Perseverance's spirits. "How does that lady do that every time?" Perseverance shook her head in wonder.

Purpose knocked on the bedroom door, "Mom, come and check me out!"

Perseverance opened her door to find Purpose twirling around in a colorful dress and her hair tied up in a neat bun. She hadn't seen Purpose this happy in a long time and was hoping Daemon would not let her down. Despite her concerns, Perseverance forced a smile.

"Purpose, you are beautiful, and I'm sure Daemon, I mean your dad, will think the same when he sees you today. Speaking of meeting your dad, we'd better get out of here soon to beat the traffic and get a good parking spot."

Purpose went back to her room to finish getting ready. As soon as Purpose ran off, Perseverance closed her bedroom door and leaned her back against it while slowly exhaling. She dropped the fake smile on her face and felt relieved to rest her jaws. She took a deep breath and dragged her feet to her closet to find something to wear.

Purpose fidgeted at her dress and nervously walked into the coffee shop to meet her biological dad. Perseverance, Michael, and Chastity found a table close by to keep a close eye on things. It was 11:00 am, the time that they were supposed to meet. Daemon was nowhere in sight. They would just have to wait for him to show.

Michael bought Perseverance a tall cup of coffee drizzled with white chocolate sauce, and fresh raspberry iced teas for him and the girls. At 11:30, Daemon still hadn't arrived. Purpose's face was no longer as bright and cheerful as when they arrived.

Frustrated, Perseverance called the number Daemon had provided, and the call went to voicemail. By noon, Purpose realized he would not show up and slowly walked to the family's table. No one knew what to say to her, so there was a long silence.

An upbeat ringtone from Perseverance's phone broke the silence – she recognized Ms. Wisdom's name on the screen.

"Hey, Ms. Wisdom! How are you doing?" Perseverance's face relaxed as she smiled at the news. She was delighted to hear Ms. Wisdom was back in the comfort of her home and was hoping for some company.

Perseverance knew visiting Ms. Wisdom would be an excellent distraction for Purpose, so she accepted the invitation. The family's overall mood instantly changed when they heard the news, and they all left the coffee shop to walk to their car.

Perseverance pulled her car into Ms. Wisdom's bumpy driveway, and the 'to-go' cup tilted over, splashing coffee on the dashboard.

"Ugh! I just cleaned this car! Purpose, do you mind asking Ms. Wisdom if she has some paper towels I could use to clean this mess up before it gets settled?"

They spied Ms. Wisdom peeking out her front window and waving. Michael looked at Perseverance and laughed, "Someone is happy to be here! And someone is happy to see us!"

Purpose leaped out of the back seat and sprung up the sidewalk towards the front door. Before Purpose could get to the top of the stairs, Ms. Wisdom opened her door and stood in the doorway with her arms wide open in anticipation of a hug. Purpose melted into Ms. Wisdom's arms, and she felt an immediate sense of peace. After the coffee shop meeting failure, Purpose needed a hug...more than she realized until that moment.

Relieved, Purpose leaned backward from the hug, "I'm so glad you are alright! Oh, my mom wants to know if you have any paper towels. She spilled coffee in her car."

Ms. Wisdom waved Purpose down the hallway, "Of course, dear, grab some off the counter in the kitchen."

Ms. Wisdom exhaled deeply as she sat down slowly in her worn-down armchair.

"Purpose, you were one of the first people I wanted to talk to when I left the hospital, so I'm glad you came over today."

Purpose reacted with curiosity. "Me? Why me?"

Ms. Wisdom replied, "I've been watching you grow up over the years, and there's something extraordinary about you. I hope you can cultivate your gifts, so I'd like you to plan our next big event. It's something special, and you are just the person to get it done right. With the doctor's orders, I can't do all I used to anymore. Are you up for the challenge?"

Honored that Ms. Wisdom would consider her for such a task, she replied, "Of course I am! Thank you, Ms. Wisdom; I needed this."

The doorbell rang, and the chime sounded off the melody of the song Amazing Grace throughout the home. Purpose laughed and said, "Only you would have a doorbell that played a melody to a song like this. Everything about you is encouraging, Ms. Wisdom."

Purpose could hear her family chattering at the front door and realized she was supposed to bring paper towels to her mother. She ran to the door with the paper towels in her hand.

"Sorry, mom, I was talking to Ms. Wisdom and forgot to bring these out."

Perseverance replied, "Don't worry about it; I found a few napkins in the glove box." She rushed inside the house to greet Ms. Wisdom. The rest of her family followed suit and found a seat on the antique, cream-colored couch in the living room next to Ms. Wisdom.

After greeting her guests warmly, Ms. Wisdom looked directly at Purpose and said, "Can you pick up that bag on the floor by the coffee table and look inside?" She pointed to a colorfully designed cloth tote bag, bulging in a few places.

Purpose looked inside and found a list of names, a brand-new planner, and other party-planning packages.

Ms. Wisdom pointed towards Purpose, "Those are for you. Contact the people whose names I listed for help with the event. The planner in there will help keep you organized. One last thing, I'd like this to be a celebration of the fruits of the spirit."

Perseverance beamed with excitement. "Wow! You'll be planning an event for the community center? Well, go ahead then, girl!" Purpose bashfully smiled while checking out her new planner.

Ms. Wisdom picked up a piece of paper and wrote Galatians Chapter 5 in a neat script with a blue pen, "Here is some homework for you, sweetheart. Study this chapter in the bible, and I know you'll figure out how to proceed afterwards."

Purpose noticed a dainty ring on Ms. Wisdom's ring finger when she reached out for the slip of paper. She thought to herself, 'That is interesting. I've never seen her with a ring on that finger before. She's been a widow for years.'

When Purpose got home, she went straight to her room to start on Ms. Wisdom's assignment. She looked at the list of names and found they were all people she had encountered at the Virtuous Community Center over the years.

She got excited, "This will be so much fun!" She turned on her desk lamp, which gave her workspace a soft glow.

As she thought about each person and her interactions, she instantly realized how they could be helpful in their unique way.

"Now, let's figure out what the fruits of the spirit are all about."

Purpose pulled out her bible and searched for Galatians 5. While reading the scripture, she found it discussed freedom granted to those who believed in Jesus when he died on the cross. As she read the chapter, she took notes in her planner and talked aloud to make sense of what she read. She removed the cap from her pen and wrote in her planning notebook:

We are not meant to be, and never will be, perfect… that's part of what is so special about Jesus dying for our sins. We have the freedom to be forgiven for our sins. Being a Christian is not just about doing our best to take part in religious acts and following commandments but expressing our faith in Jesus by showing love towards one another.

She thought to herself, "Okay, this part makes sense. My mother always tells me to treat people how I'd like to be treated...with love and respect. I get this part, but what about the fruits of the spirit? Ms. Wisdom said that's the theme of this event, and I have to understand this for the event to turn out perfectly."

She began to worry. Self-doubt crept in, making her wonder if she could pull this event together.

Suddenly, she overheard her mother yell, "Don't play with my daughter's emotions, Daemon!" Perseverance was stomping up the hall while having a heated conversation on the phone with Daemon.

Purpose realized her mother was angry about what happened earlier in the day.

"I can't believe he didn't show up after making such a big deal about spending time with me the other day." Purpose muttered while shrugging her shoulders. She felt deflated, and her posture went from upward and confident to slumped over and discouraged. The creative energy she had was slowly dissipating.

She put on her earphones, found her favorite music playlist on her phone, and tuned out her mother and the rest of the world. Thankful for the uplifting distraction, she turned the page of her bible and kept reading until she got to Galatians 5:22. "Aha! The fruits of the spirit!"

She read out loud, "But the fruit of the spirit is love, joy, peace, patience, kindness, goodness, and faithfulness." She thought about what she had just read and continued to write in her planner.

> *Fruits are a part of a plant that produces seeds spread throughout the land. The type of fruit that grows depends on what type of plant produces its seed. If you receive Jesus into your heart and allow the Holy Spirit to guide you, the fruits of the spirit (love, joy, peace, patience, kindness, goodness, and faithfulness) will manifest in your life. It will show in the things you do and how you treat people around you.*

After re-reading her notes, Purpose thought about her life and how she thought the Galatians scripture could apply. She was angry and disappointed in her biological father and what happened today. "It's not okay for him to treat me wrong, but I will not spend my time being angry at him forever. If I ever get a chance to see him, I'll try to be kind."

Purpose felt she better understood the meaning of the event that Ms. Wisdom asked her to plan. After a bit of brainstorming, she came up with a name for the event, *A Fruit Harvest Festival*.

Purpose clinched her fists and joyfully screeched out loud. She picked up her phone and started to contact the people on the list Ms. Wisdom had provided. Her productivity shed a little sunshine on the gloomy day.

"How are we coming up with enough money to keep the community center open? Ms. Wisdom just got out of the hospital, and I don't want to bother her with anything stressful. Besides, I'm sure that she's aware of things. Maybe that was causing her health issues in the first place?" Purpose overheard her mother whispering on the phone as she walked towards the kitchen.

When Perseverance realized Purpose was in the kitchen, she quickly ended her phone call. Purpose grabbed a bowl out of the cabinet and hesitated to say anything but eventually said, "Mom, is everything okay with the community center?"

Perseverance sighed and said, "Sweetheart, to be honest, no, it isn't. We have so little time to keep the doors open. I'm trying to figure out how to help save this place that has been a beacon of love in our community."

Purpose poured cereal into her bowl, the box mid-air as she thought of a plan.

"Mom, I spent last night working on the event that Ms. Wisdom wants me to put together, and I think this could be a great opportunity to pull the community together to help save the center. I'm supposed to hold our first meeting at the community center after school. I can bring it up to everyone then."

Perseverance looked at her daughter and smiled.

"It sounds like Ms. Wisdom chose the right person to pull this event off after all!"

Purpose smiled back, feeling valued by her mom and Ms. Wisdom. Purpose spent every moment she could throughout the day rehearsing what she would say at the meeting. The closer it got to the meeting start time, the more nervous she became, but her feelings were overshadowed by her determination to help keep the community center open.
Perseverance drove Purpose to the Virtuosities Community Center an hour before the meeting and assisted with setting up the conference room. She was excited and nervous for her daughter and said a silent prayer.

"Lord, please help this be a successful turnout for my baby girl. She needs this right now. We all do in our own way."

Perseverance looked at the clock on the wall and quickly headed to her car to grab a box of muffins she had bought for the meeting.

"Thank you all for meeting with me today! You were all personally chosen by Ms. Wisdom to be a part of this event. She wanted you to know she is grateful for you all and happy you want to be a part of something that means so much to her but, most importantly, offers so much to our community."

Purpose greeted everyone in the conference room as though she was a professional just putting together another large event. She continued, "Let's first see who is here and then figure out how we will get this done with the short time we have."

Purpose read off the sign-in sheet, "Charity, Honesty, Courage, Harmony, my Mom – Perseverance, and Chastity. Thank you so much for being here today and being part of the planning committee!"

Purpose continued by explaining the event's theme and sharing what she learned while reading chapter five in Galatians. Before assigning roles, Purpose took a moment to share the dreadful news about the financial troubles the center was having. By the time the meeting ended, they had developed a plan to raise money for the community center…while pulling off the special event for Ms. Wisdom.

For the next few weeks, Perseverance saw the event committee members spend countless hours at the community center after school. Charity was able to use the skills she learned while completing her community service hours to help with fundraising activities. She set up a booth after school every day and was joined by her sister, Honesty, and their mother.

In a few weeks, they raised $1,500 to keep the community center open and sell tickets for the fundraising event. When the three of them shared their testimony about how the Virtuous Community

Center played a critical role in restoring their relationships and getting them on track toward success, they inspired the people who visited their booth to help keep the doors open by donating money.

Courage convinced her soccer team to help with car washing events to raise money for the community center. It surprised her to see the teammate that had once bullied her, Tina, step up to the plate. Tina was usually the first to arrive and the last to leave, and throughout the process, the two of them built a foundation for a friendship. During one of the car washing events, Ms. Wisdom showed up to express her gratitude and handed out her famous Proverbs 31:25 tee shirts.

Harmony was busy filling the auditorium with songs of praise while orchestrating a choir full of kids from the local area. Since Harmony lived a few blocks from the community center, she convinced kids to join the choir. Many of the kids she grew up with never knew that Harmony had a passion for singing until she started helping Ms. Wisdom out by singing at a few events. The opportunities to sing helped build her confidence, and she was a role model for other kids who aspired to sing. Many kids who looked up to her were glad to sing with her.

Harmony's grandfather, Mr. Johnson, continued to serve as facilities caretaker by keeping the grass cut and neatly edged, the bathrooms cleaned, and the hallways freshly mopped and smelling like bleach. When he wasn't taking care of janitorial duties, he spent time with Ms. Wisdom.

People asked Harmony what was happening between the two, but she would just reply with a sneaky grin and shrug, "That's their business. You will be the first to know when they want to make it your business."

Perseverance continued to care for business affairs while teaching the teen and teen-mother classes. Chastity volunteered to help with the teen classes after she completed her homework in the break room. After facing her challenges with abstaining from sex, Chastity had a new appreciation for listening to her mother talk to other young ladies about self-love, self-preservation, and making sweet lemonade from life's lemons. Chastity also spent time decorating the center for the upcoming event and assisting with ticket sales.

It was a week before the event, and Purpose was excited to see how things were falling into place. She had the perfect team helping her, and each was as invested in keeping the community center's doors open. They worked long hours during school nights and had loads of parental support.

Ms. Wisdom entered the room at the last meeting before the event, surprising everyone. She was accompanied by Mr. Johnson and dressed in a bright summer dress. Everyone greeted Ms. Wisdom, who was back to her usual energetic self.

Ms. Wisdom lifted her arms and said, "Ladies, I

just wanted to stop by to tell you I truly appreciate your hard work. No matter what happens at the Fruit Harvest Festival next week, just know that you've already made me very proud. Each one of you!"

Mr. Johnson left the room and returned with a few boxes of pizza and soda cans. "I'm sure you all are hungry after a day of school and work, so here's a little something for your stomachs." Ms. Wisdom walked around the room to hug everyone and left so everyone could return to work.

The week before the Fruit Harvest Festival sped by, and donations continued to pour in. It was now Friday – the day before the event. Perseverance stayed late in the office to complete some last-minute tasks on her to-do list.

She unlocked the donation box and began tallying up the money. She was elated the event committee managed to raise $25,000 so far. Just $5,000 short of the amount needed to keep the community center's doors open.

She placed the money in a white envelope and wrote the amount outside with a black pen on the flap. She wrapped a large rubber band around the envelope, placed it in the dark grey safe hidden in the wall closet, and updated the spreadsheet tracking the community center's budget. Her eyes began to sting as tears of relief rolled down her left, then right cheek.

She whispered, "I'm so proud of my baby girl. I'm so proud of us all. Thank you, God, for everything that you are doing. You are so faithful!" She turned off the computer, grabbed her belongings, and turned out the office light before locking up the building.

Purpose woke up to feelings she did not anticipate on the big event day. She lay in her bed, overwhelmed with nervousness. She was worried the event would not go as planned and she would let everyone down. She felt nauseous, and stomach acid crept up her throat." I think I'm going to throw up," she thought.

Perseverance walked into Purpose's bedroom and sang, "Good morning! It's the big day today!" She pulled the cover from her daughter's head and saw her baggy eyes. "My goodness, did you get any sleep last night?" She walked over to the window to open the curtains and let some sunlight into the room.

Purpose pulled the covers back over her head and said, "Mom, can you take it from here? I'm exhausted and don't think I can do anything else."

Perseverance sat on her daughter's bed, "Don't be silly, sweetheart, the hard part is over. All you have to do is show up and enjoy watching everything fall into place. Remember, you have a great team, and everyone is in this together. It will be fine."

Perseverance went to the bathroom and returned with a warm face towel. She gently rubbed the towel over Purpose's face, "This should get your day started, and now you have one less thing to do."

Purpose laughed and said, "Thanks, Mom," and rolled out of her bed to get dressed. She was glad that the event committee voted to wear shirts that Ms. Wisdom had custom-made for them, paired with black skirts to the Fruit Harvest Festival, eliminating the stress of figuring out what to wear for the day. She pulled the bright white shirt with pink letters from her closet and admired the words spelling out 'Little Virtuosities' across the front.

When the family pulled into the Virtuous Community Center's parking lot, Perseverance saw the committee members had arrived early and had hung a larger banner with the words 'Fruit Harvest Festival' in bold print. Colorful balloons outlined the entranceway of the community center and danced in the wind as they welcomed everyone who walked through the doors. Purpose darted out of the back seat, excited for her team's progress, "I'll meet you guys inside!"

When Purpose walked inside the community center, she was glad to see that members of the event committee were taking care of their assigned tasks just as she had envisioned. She was also happy to see some guests had arrived and were walking around admiring the decorations, which embraced the event's theme of the harvesting of fruit.

As the guests walked throughout the community center, they realized the theme was not based on fruits meant to be consumed but the fruits of the spirit, as depicted in Galatians 5:22, which was precisely what Ms. Wisdom had hoped. The center had festive displays that creatively captured glimpses of love, joy, peace, patience, kindness, goodness, and faithfulness, demonstrated in various forms by the community center's staff and volunteers. There were heartwarming pictures of homeless people being served hot plates of food on tables draped with lovely tablecloths, children being provided with school backpacks, and Ms. Wisdom being embraced with hugs that overflowed with gratitude for her service to the community.

Purpose was speechless. She thought, "This is even better than I imagined it would be." After admiring the work, she rushed to the back office to place her belongings away so she could help.

Perseverance, Michael, and Charity walked through the front entrance of the community center and were greeted by lively music and cheerful chatter. The bass boom from the live music the musicians played on stage echoed throughout the halls of the community center. Speakers were placed throughout the auditorium so each guest could fully enjoy the live piano, guitar, drums, and saxophone played by the musicians.

Perseverance was delighted to see guests smiling and wiggling their bodies to the beat of the music. The smell of freshly baked fruit pies, muffins, brownies, and fresh apple cider filled the room. Love was in the air. This event had the largest turnout Perseverance had attended over the years, and she was so proud that everyone helped pull things together. She noticed the fundraising table was swarmed by people donating money to keep the center's doors open.

Perseverance looked at Michael and said, "Things are going to be alright." Michael nodded in agreement, "Yes, love, it will certainly be alright," and leaned in to hug her.

The event started with the sweet songs of praise from Harmony and the choir she led. Many eyes were misty with tears, moved by the sweet notes and words. The event showcased people's talents throughout the community, and each presentation was creatively themed around the fruits of the spirit. The event kept attendees engaged.

While a young ladies were wrapping up their dance routine on stage, Perseverance saw Daemon come in through the back door. She nudged Michael with her elbow, "Michael, what is he doing here? How did he find out about this?"

Michael gulped, "I told him about it when he called to see if he could reschedule his meet-up with Purpose. I am so sorry; it slipped my mind – I think I got distracted minutes after the call. I honestly didn't think he would show up."

"I'll talk to him. Don't worry about it," Michael whispered to Perseverance, then walked toward Daemon.

Michael caught Daemon, flowers in his hands, as he was inching closer to the stage. The applause and clapping were so loud Daemon asked Michael to step outside to talk.

When they got outside, Michael saw Daemon was not in his usual defensive stance and said, "Hey man, what's going on?"

Daemon replied, "I need to apologize for not showing up the other day." His shoulders slumped, and he could hardly look Michael in the face. Daemon paused and looked away from Michael to gather his composure. He was clearly going through some emotional turmoil. He continued, "I didn't know what to say to her, man. We all know how badly I treated Perseverance after I found out she was pregnant. I wasn't there. I didn't care to be there. How do I answer that?"

Another round of applause erupted through the cracked doors.

Michael looked at Daemon and said, "How about you just be there? That's all that matters right now. We will not get in your way if you want a healthy relationship with Purpose. On the other hand, if you are going to mistreat her as you did her mother, you better walk away now. We won't stand by and allow you to hurt her."

Daemon looked at Michael and handed him the flowers, "Please give these to her and tell her I'm proud of her. I realize I'm just not ready to do this yet."

Michael gave Daemon a stern look and said, "This is probably the best conversation we've ever had since I met you in that high school parking lot, Daemon." Michael nodded at Daemon, "Let me know when you're ready. I ask that you keep things calm and cordial when you talk to my wife. She's already been through enough. I'm not sure why you're upset with her in the first place."

Daemon exhaled, his shoulders slumping even lower, "Okay, I can work on that. Thanks, man." He shook his head and looked away but noted before he turned away, "Thanks for being the father to her that I could not be."

Michael smiled and reached out to shake Daemon's hand. "I appreciate that."

The music lightened up, and Purpose gracefully walked on stage. Purpose spoke eloquently while she thanked everyone for their support and shared a few words about how much the Virtuous Community Center meant to her. She then shared the event's significance and explained in more detail why they were celebrating the 'fruits of the spirit.'

Purpose then asked everyone to warmly welcome Ms. Wisdom, who humbly took command of the stage. Ms. Wisdom seemed frail and much older than she was when she started the community center. The audience graciously extended their applause to accommodate her feeble steps toward the podium.

"Thank you, everyone; I'd like to first give all the glory and honor to God, who is the head of my life." She then talked through a slideshow highlighting significant moments at the community center over the years. On her last slide, she added, "I'd like to ask the planning committee of today's event to join me on the stage."

"Purpose, Charity, Honesty, Courage, Harmony, Perseverance, and Chastity…" Everyone rose to their feet as they walked up to the stage and provided thunderous applause. "I single-handedly chose these spectacular ladies to plan this event for a reason. Each of these young ladies walks a life filled with the fruits of the spirit in their unique way. They have shown their love for others and our community through tireless work to pull together today's event. To celebrate their accomplishments, I have a special presentation."

Ms. Wisdom asked the planning committee to step to the side. "I'd like to present to you all the Little Virtuosities Wall of Fame!" she shouted as she pulled back a curtain, revealing candid pictures of each of the young ladies.

"A virtuous woman knows her worth, far beyond precious rubies. She's fearless and has a firm foundation in faith and love. She embraces her community. Please join me in encouraging these ladies to continue to make a difference, one virtue at a time!"

She walked towards Perseverance and said, "I have one last special announcement. One of the important things about fruit is that it produces seeds that spread throughout the land. With that said, I am stepping down from my role to make room for Perseverance to take over management of the center and produce new fruit. She's been doing an amazing job the past few months. I will continue to serve as a consultant, but the Virtuous Community Center is in excellent hands."

Speechless, Perseverance's mouth dropped. She was so shocked she nearly tripped over her feet as she hugged Ms. Wisdom. The attendees cheered and clapped their hands. Many were personally on the receiving end of community service and knew Perseverance was a perfect choice. As Perseverance hugged Ms. Wisdom, she cried tears of joy. Harmony ended the presentation portion of the event by singing a song.

As people mingled with one another throughout the community center, Michael approached Purpose and handed her the flowers from Daemon.

Purpose smiled and said, "Thank you!"

Michael whispered, "They're from Daemon."

Surprised, Purpose's eyes widened, and her head whipped around, looking for her biological father, "What? Wait! Is he here?"

Michael nodded and said, "He was here, but he didn't stay. He wanted you to know he was proud of you and is sorry for not showing up the other day. He hopes to have another chance when the time is right."

Purpose smiled and said, "Okay, that would be nice." She gazed at Michael and smiled. "I am so glad you are in my life. Whatever happens, I'll always have you as my real dad."

Purpose's words warmed Michael's heart. He grinned back at her.

Purpose was eager to see what was in her goodie bag, so she asked Michael to hold her flowers. She saw a gold envelope with beautifully-embossed embroidery on the front.

She peeped inside and saw a wedding announcement.

"Wait a minute... Ms. Wisdom and Mr. Johnson are getting married! I knew something was going on between those two!" she grinned.

She looked across the room, saw the pair holding hands, and made eye contact with Ms. Wisdom. By the looks on Purposes' face, Ms. Wisdom knew she saw the wedding invitation and winked.

Little Virtuosities

222

About the Author

Shira Amour

The author is a full-time, working mother and wife who pursues her writing career in the evenings and weekends. She received her bachelor's degree in Human Development with a focus in Adolescents which enables her to psychologically understand how adolescents develop, grow, and change – mentally and physically. She attended theology school for spiritual development and obtained her Master's degree in Public Administration to facilitate programs that help people realize their potential.

She was introduced to poetry while in elementary school, sparking her passion for writing. Her love of poetry, the support of kind-hearted people, and her personal relationship with God helped her become more than a conqueror. While growing up, she experienced many hardships and gravitated to writing poetry to express herself and process the challenges she encountered.

She uses her personal experiences, memories, interactions, and life solutions to teach lessons in her stories. She writes about subjects relevant to adolescents for positive impact and shares her knowledge in story format to help them overcome their challenges.

Media Links

Interested in being a part of a community that provides tools and resources to help young ladies realize their internal and external beauty?

Visit the Little Virtuosities' website to learn more about us, and to find links to motivational videos, blogs, merchandise, and other inspirational resources. Subscribe to our newsletter and social media sites to receive direct access to the latest updates and words of encouragement.

Website:

https://www.littlevirtuosities.com/

YouTube:

https://youtube.com/@littlevirtuosities6884

Merchandise:

https://www.littlevirtuosities.com/shop

About the Book

Do you spend a lot of time focusing on your external beauty…what you're going to wear, your hairstyle, or make-up? Many of us want to look good and take pride in how we look – there is nothing wrong with that.

What happens when you are faced with a storm that requires more than an umbrella and trendy raincoat to survive? Taking time to develop internally will better prepare you to endure the challenges you may face in life.

You're invited to join Courage, Harmony, Purpose, and other young ladies as they embark on their journey to navigate their lives and weather the storms of teen struggles. The experiences these young ladies encounter are reflective of modern-day dilemmas such as suicide ideations, bullying, and online dating.

During this journey, you are sure to discover helpful characteristics and solutions to apply to your life circumstances. The lessons learned by the young ladies in this book will help readers realize within themselves and their lives tools to help overcome negative life issues and inspiration to develop strength, resiliency, and internal beauty.

Made in the USA
Las Vegas, NV
19 February 2023

67792741R00132